# Evangeline

# Evangeline

## A Novel

### Finis Fox

PELICAN PUBLISHING COMPANY
Gretna 1999

*The word "Pelican" and the depiction of a pelican are
trademarks of Pelican Publishing Company, Inc., and are
registered in the U.S. Patent and Trademark Office.*

**Library of Congress Cataloging-in-Publication Data**

Fox, Finis.
    [Romance of Evangeline]
    Evangeline : a novel / by Finis Fox. - 1st Pelican
    Pouch ed.
       p.    cm.
    Based on the poem by Longfellow.
    Originally published as: The romance of
    Evangeline. 1929.
    ISBN 1-56554-658-X (pbk. : alk. paper)
    1. Acadians—History—Fiction.  I. Longfellow,
Henry Wadsworth, 1807-1882.  Evangeline.
II. Title.
PS3511.09644R66  1999
813'.52-dc21                98-56125
                      CIP

Printed in Canada

Published by Pelican Publishing Company, Inc.
1000 Burmaster Street, Gretna, Louisiana 70053

# THE ROMANCE OF
# EVANGELINE

## CHAPTER I

### THE LAND OF ACADIE

The last days of August had come to the
gently sloping valleys of Nova Scotia. Already the blue haze of Indian summer hung
lazily in the sky, so low in places that it
seemed for all the world like smoke, rising
from long, orderly rows of Indian lodges
—that were not lodges at all, but great,
golden, shocks of ripening grain, marching
away over hill and dale until they were
lost among the apple orchards that bordered
the sea, where the restless tides of the Bay
of Fundy bit into the Basin of Minas, only
to be turned back by the dikes of the Acadian farmers.

Quail called from the stubble. In the
apple orchards, the droning of bees and the
soft murmuring of the branches, stirring
gently in the cool, invigorating wind, fresh

1

from the long reaches of the sea, broke the stillness of noonday. Inland, where the valleys swelled away to hills, great, unbroken forests of pine and hemlock brooded dark and forbidding, the chattering of squirrels and busy purring of an unseen brook, splashing over moss-covered rocks in its headlong flight to the ocean, awakened echoes that sounded and resounded eerily in the deep silence of the woods.

To-day a man, a boy only, picked his way across the fields. Wherever bush or tree offered a shady respite from the sun, he stopped to refresh himself. He was a tall, handsome youth, his dark eyes and softly curling hair as black as midnight. He was Baptiste Leblanc, the notary's son, from Grand-Pré. He was attired in his Sunday-best to-day, for this was no casual visit that he was about. As he lingered in the grateful shade of a wild-cherry tree, he carefully dusted the large silver buckles that adorned his boots and adjusted for the twentieth time his lace cuffs and tie. From where he stood, he could see the white spire of the church in Grand-Pré. He seemed to take courage from it, and with renewed eagerness, climbed the hill toward a great, rambling farm-house.

A sturdy house it was, firmly built with

rafters of oak and great, hand-hewn beams, surmounted on either end by huge chimneys of native stone that roared out a mighty defiance in winter-time to the howling gales and relentless blizzards of the Northland. It asked no quarter from either wind or storm. Pegged together and nailed down with hand-wrought nails made by Gabriel Lajeunesse at his forge in Grand-Pré, the home of Benedict Bellefontaine had stood for twenty years, watching the sea with one eye and guarding the valleys of Acadie with the other.

The muscle of men, and something of the stout heart of its master, had gone into its making. With its huge barns and houses for the fowl and livestock, it squatted four-square like a feudal castle among its rich fields and heavily-laden orchards.

It seemed so secure, so unassailable, that unconsciously Baptiste stayed his steps as he neared it. Of a sudden, his mission took on new significance and became a momentuous undertaking. His hand trembled as he asked himself what reason he had for hoping to find the heart of Evangeline Bellefontaine, Benedict's daughter, easier of conquest than this formidable house of which she was mistress. Back in Grand-Pré, safe in the snug shelter of his home, he had felt confident of himself, but now a growing uneasiness gripped him, and he drew a bucket of water from the moss-covered well at which he had stopped and quaffed it eagerly. Far afield, he could see the men, busy at their work, and he raised his hand to shade his eyes, trying to discover if Benedict was with his men.

He fancied he saw him, standing beside a broad-wheeled wain, and he heaved a sigh of relief. Surely the fortress could be easier attacked with the master away. Squaring his shoulders with new determination, he quickly passed the sheep fold and found a winding path, lined with hollyhocks and sun-flowers, that wound past quaint dove côtes, and into the yard.

The doves quit cooing as he passed, and Baptiste glanced up at them nervously and fancied they looked down disapprovingly at him. For a moment, he was at the point of fleeing unceremoniously. Courage came to him, however, and his mouth straightened bravely.

"No," he murmured, "I will not go, I shall ask her if it kills me!"

It was so peaceful and quiet beneath the old sycamore, whose spreading branches formed a leafy canopy over the thatched roof and dormer windows that his voice boomed in his ears, and he looked about quickly to see if he had been observed. Then, strangely, enough, he smiled at his own fears. He had been there so often, and always so kindly received that his present anxiety suddenly became something to be ashamed of. His eyes roamed from the old door with its heavy knocker and iron hinges, rusted now by snow and rain, to the beehives under the sycamore, overhung with a penthouse such as one sees over road-side shrines of the Blessed Virgin in remote parts of Normandy, and back to the wood-bine which rambled and twined about the trellised portico.

Truly it was far from being a forbidding aspect. And yet, thought Baptiste, how in-finitely less lovely than she who dwelt here. To win her, to claim her hand, that indeed were heaven. He crossed himself, as though enlisting the aid of the Almighty in his be-half. Fear was behind him now. What could life ask of him that he would not dare for her?

Uplifted and ennobled by his great love for Evangeline, he raised the knocker and let it clang bravely. Breathlessly he waited for the door to open, and in his eagerness wondered which sounded the louder, the clanging of the knocker or the beating of his heart.

Minutes passed, and he received no answer. He opened the door at last and stepped in, sweeping the room with his dark eyes. He was about to call out when the sharp, staccato pit-a-pat of quaint wooden shoes reached his ear from the direction of the kitchen, furnishing an obligato to the gay little melody Evangeline hummed as she worked.

"It is she!" Baptiste murmured, and he paused to listen as her voice rose in the lilting strains of *"En roulant ma bolue."* The old folk-song swept him along with its merry rhythm, and he caught himself keeping time as she sang:

"Derrière chez nous, y a-t-un étang,
  Enroulant ma boule.
  Trois beaux canards s'en vont baignant,
  En roulant ma boule.
  Rouli, Roulant, ma boule roulante,
  En roulant ma boule roulante,
  En roulant ma boule roulante."

The song stopped without warning and the sound of a crashing plate reached Baptiste's ears, followed a second later by a sharp *"Mon Dieu!"* A few moments and

the song was resumed. Baptiste breathed
easier and quietly crossed the living room,
slipped by the old grandfather clock and
leaned against the open doorway of the
kitchen. Unseen, he feasted his eyes upon
Evangeline as she mixed a mass of batter
in a huge copper bowl using a spoon so
cumbersome that it seemed out of all pro-
portion to her dainty hands.

The appetizing aroma of hot bread
reached Baptiste's nostrils, and he
breathed deeply as he saw the long, brown
loaves that covered one end of the table.
Benedict Bellefontaine was the wealthiest
of all the Acadian farmers, but still he toiled
from dawn till dark, and it never occurred
to Evangeline that she shouldn't do the
same. There were many mouths to feed at
this season of the year, so she had been busy
for hours. But the bread-making was over.
The batter she was so busily mixing now
was not intended ever to tickle the palates
of her father's laborers.

Baptiste had often seen her in church on
Sunday mornings, demure in a Norman cap
and kirtle of blue, the fairest of all the
maidens in the village of Grand-Pré, an
ethereal beauy in her face and a glow of
the spirituelle in her eyes as she knelt and
devoutly blessed herself. But here in her

kitchen, busy with her housewifely duties, was a new Evangeline, and Baptiste couldn't have told which he preferred.

He was a thrifty lad, as one had to be in Acadie, and this well-ordered kitchen, flanked with its groaning shelves of jellies and jams and other toothsome sweets, laid away against the long winter so soon to come, doubly assured Baptiste that Evangeline was an incomparable jewel among girls, whose equal was not to be found in all Acadie.

A sigh escaped his lips as he reluctantly reminded himself that he was only one of many admiring youths who worshipped her as the saint of his deepest devotion.

Guiltily, he started from his romantic reverie and, in boyish embarrassment, called out from the door, "Evangeline!"

His cry startled her. The big spoon dropped from her fingers. Then her dark eyes flashed a welcome but as she recognized Bapiste, the eagerness died out of her eyes. It was as though she had expected to find another than René Leblanc's son facing her.

An unconscious sigh escaped her lips. There was deep disappointment in it, and then, suddenly afraid that Baptiste might read her secret, she turned for a quick glance at her oven. She was smiling gaily when she faced him again and gave him a curtsy.

"It is good to see you again, Baptiste," she said simply, trying to make her words glow with the warmth and hospitality always shown a guest in Acadie. She remarked his dress then, and sudden apprehension gripped her. "What has happened, Baptiste—your father?"

Bapiste glanced down at his ruffles and silver buckles, and shook his head in growing embarrassment. "My father is not sick; it was not that that brought me."

It was not necessary for him to say more; Evangeline's worst fears were confirmed. She picked up her spoon before Baptiste could get it for her, and bending over her mixing bowl stirred the batter furiously to hide her own confusion.

"Sit down, Baptiste," she murmured, without looking up, and motioned to a stool in the corner of the kitchen near a window-box, fragrant with late summer flowers. "I will be finished soon. See, I am baking cookies as a surprise for . . . " she hesitated for a moment, "a surprise for my father."

With open adoration, Baptiste's eyes followed Evangeline as she chatted lightly with him, rolled out the dough, cut the cookies into odd shapes, and slipped them into the cavernous mouth of the huge oven.

Silently he admired her ability to appear so casual, a gift he would have given anything to possess at this moment. A studious young man, preparing to follow the footsteps of his father, the honored notary of Grand-Pré, Baptiste was more thoroughly versed in the intricacy of the law than in the art of courtship.

Only a short while ago he had crossed the meadows leading into Benedict Bellefontaine's yard, courageous of heart, with words of love fairly tumbling from his lips. But now, in her presence, he felt hopelessly lost. The glowing phrases he had planned vanished into thin air, and only his eloquent eyes were spokesmen for his ardor as they followed her about, enchanted by the willowy suppleness of her figure, the graceful slope of her shoulders, her arms tapering to delicate wrists, her slender throat above the rippling lace of her collar, her eyes flashing beneath her long, drooping lashes.

His silence became greater with the passing minutes. Evangeline tried for the tenth time to turn the conversation into easier channels.

"Do you think I will make a good cook?"

she challenged gaily, as she bent over the oven to peek at her cookies, turning a crisp, golden brown.

"Perhaps, you are practicing to be a good wife?" Baptiste tried to speak in jest, but the tremor in his voice betrayed the secret thought that lay near his heart.

Evangeline glanced up quickly. With a woman's unerring intuition, she sensed that Baptiste would say what he had come to say, and that he would not be turned from the purpose of his visit, so she pretended an efficient industry, finding innumerable, fanciful little things about the kitchen that demanded her immediate attention, pleased that he should want her, and yet distressed because she must refuse him.

Persistently Baptiste followed her about, not certain in his own mind whether she was encouraging him or trying to avoid him. Busily she fluttered to a high shelf to put away some spices. As she reached up to replace the canister, Baptiste caught her hand and tried to draw her to him. Nervously she looked about for some plausible escape. Then she sniffed suspiciously.

"Oh, Baptiste! The cookies!" She dashed to the oven and, with her apron, lifted the pan just in time to save them from burning ... and to save herself from an equally difficult situation.

Instantly Baptiste was at her side, whiffing the delicious aromas that permeated the kitchen. "They are perfect!" he exclaimed, "even as ..." Evangeline, afraid to have him go on, caught up a big pewter pitcher and tripped over to the window boxes to water her flowers.

The afternoon sun, streaming through the latticed windows, glinted fitfully on her raven hair, parted in the middle and lying close to her head, a wealth of it falling over her shoulders in two lustrous braids. In the olive complexion of her face, the exquisite arch of her eyebrows, the vivacious curve of her mouth, the sparkling pools in her eyes, her French ancestry was vividly etched.

Baptiste followed her. He found his tongue at last.

"Evangeline, I have always loved you ... "

At the sound of his abrupt declaration, Evangeline turned from her flowers and gazed at him. There was an unuttered fervency and longing in his vibrant voice. It was not what he had said. Other youths in the village had vowed their love in more eloquent terms; but there was such an air of dependence and desperation in his simple declaration that Evangeline was convinced of the futility of further pursuing an evasive course. She liked this handsome son of René LeBlanc, and admired him. She knew that his love was sincere, and she did not wish to hurt him.

"You are my life, Evangeline! I worship you. I adore you." His words now came thick and fast. His hands clasped hers, and he bent over her, his eyes searching eagerly for a responsive answer.

Evangeline could not answer at once. It grew very quiet in the old farm-house. Second after second slipped away, forging its own answer. Baptiste's face became haggard looking. In his heart he knew he had lost.

"But Evangeline . . ." he began.

"I am sorry, Baptiste," she stopped him before he could pour out the full yearning of his intense love for her, "but there is room in my heart for only one love."

She paused for a moment. Baptiste's lips curled in a tragic attempt to smile.

"And that is for another . . ."

A dark shadow spread over Baptiste's face. His eyes moistened with tears. Vainly he tried to fight them back. He felt her hand touch his with an indefinable gentleness, an innate tenderness that had healed the wounds of other rejected suitors and made friends of them for life.

The room became close, hot, stifling. The spinning wheel near the fireplace, the long row of copper pots, the antique chairs and huge carved table, swam before him.

"I—I wish you happiness, Evangeline… always," he stammered briefly with choking voice. Then he slowly turned and stalked blindly from the room.

Wistfully, Evangeline followed him with misty eyes as he passed down the path that lead to the stile. In her heart surged a poignant pity that she could not return his love. In her ears lingered his stammered, unselfish words:

"I wish you happiness, Evangeline . . . always!"

# CHAPTER II

## "IT IS GABRIEL!"

The long afternoon had worn away. Up in her attic bedroom, quaintly furnished and overhung with a low beamed ceiling, Evangeline arose from her spinning wheel and darted to a dormer window overlooking the sea. Pulling aside the dimity curtains, she peered out and scanned the horizon. A shadow of disappointment crossed her face. With a petulant pout and a shug of her shoulders, she returned to her work, absently humming snatches of gay little songs as her foot worked the treadle and her hands dexterously handled the distaff. Restless, eyes aglow with expectancy, she was soon at the window again.

At last a sail, small and indistinct in the hazy distance, rewarded her and brought a radiant flush to her cheeks. Quickly she dashed to her mirror to tuck a few stray curls under her cap.

"It's Gabriel!" she murmured, and then, arrested by her excitement, she sighed,

"Help me, Holy Mother of God! I never knew love could be like this."

She kicked off her wooden sabots and sent them flying over the winding staircase. The wooden shoes sailed into the great living-room and miraculously missed the hoary head of her father as he entered the house.

Startled out of his revierie by this unceremonious reception, Benedict drew back and glanced up just in time to see Evangeline scurrying into her room. He smiled to himself, and to confirm his thought, he stepped to the door and swept the sea with his eyes. He saw the small fishing smack that had so excited his daughter. He nodded as he glimpsed it. "Gabriel," he mused, apparently well pleased that it should be the son of Basil, the smith of Grand-Pré, whose coming brought the color of roses to his daughter's cheeks.

There was a bond between these two fathers that harked back to the days of their youth, when these very acres, that now were ripe with grain, had stood under water, where the tides played at will. In that day, Grand-Pré had been only a huddle of huts, made of straw and rushes. The pinch of poverty was on everyone.

Many had laughed when Benedict Bellefontaine had first suggested the building of a dike to keep out the restless tides of the Basin of Minas and reclaim that vast swamp, green and lush to the eye, but knee-deep in water.

Basil, the blacksmith, had not laughed. He was a mighty man, even then, wide of girth and with the arm of a giant. Together they had floundered around belly-deep in the water, planning their dike that was to make Acadie a land of plenty.

They had little to work with. The tools and necessities of the mason were missing, so they had recourse to nothing better than crude *aboteaux* of trees and brush. They made great baskets of willows, towed them where they were needed and filled them with stones unil they rested on the bottom of the sea. Other baskets were placed on top of them. Clay was tamped down into the crevices.

Gradually the dike took form. The scoffers were routed. Night and day men watched that dike of mud for the tiniest opening. The sea gave up grudgingly, trying their patience sore. Then it was that Benedict had solved the riddle of making bricks.

Father Felician, the curé, had called them together on the sand and gave thanks to

God for this direct manifestation of His divine approval.

The dike was faced with bricks. The flood-gates were made, and the sea was tamed at last. Slowly the water drained away. Basil tempered a ploughshare, and the first furrow was turned up. The soil was black and rich.

Benedict nodded to himself as he recalled that day. The promise of that furrow of fine black loam had been fullfilled. All morning long he had ridden through golden fields where his harvesters were reaping the crops, over green meadows where his cattle grazed by the hundred, over grassy hillsides where shepherds watched his flocks. And every inch of it had been won from the sea, bringing prosperity and plenty not only to him but to the whole vale of the Gaspereau. And Basil's heart and hand were in it, even as were his own.

And now what greater blessing to either than that the son of one should take to wife the motherless daughter of the other?

Benedict wiped a tear from his eye as he turned from the window. He had hardly regained his usual composure when Evangeline sailed down the stairs, her feet encased in dainty black slippers.

She flashed him a smile, and waving a

blithe farewell, tried to slip out of the door. Benedict caught her and drew her into his arms.

"I'm in a great hurry, father," Evangeline pleaded.

"Yes?" he teased. "Where is it you go in such haste? Is some one ill, my child? But no! That would not account for the roses in your cheeks."

Evangeline snuggled close to him and with her face buried on his bosom, whispered, "Gabriel—he is coming home."

Benedict held her off at arm's length and smiled tenderly at her. "So it's Gabriel, eh? Well—run along—and bring him home with you!"

Evangeline was gone on the instant, crossing the yard at a bound.

Hurriedly she ran over the stile and down the path toward the sea, her heart beating in wild excitement. Suddenly she sighted white-haired Father Felician, the curé of the parish, coming up from the village, a spiritual figure in his ministerial robes of black and crucifix of shining silver.

He waved to her. "I'll surely be late," she protested. But she dared not go on without stopping for Father Felician's blessing.

She hesitated indecisively, glancing uncertainly down toward the sea, then back to the curé as he smiled a benign greeting. Quickly she ran forward and dropped on her knees before him.

"Bless me, Father . . . quick!" she breathlessly exclaimed as she cast down her eyes and bent her head in reverence.

Bewildered, the old priest looked down at the kneeling girl. No sooner had he blessed her than she was up and away. He watched her as she dashed toward the shore, unable to understand the reason for her strange conduct—and thinking something was surely amiss, started to follow her.

Nearing the rocky caverns of the Basin of Minas, sails full in the breeze, the fishing smack plunged through the white caps.

Clinging to the mast was a stalwart youth of heroic mold and romantic mood, his chestnut hair flying in the wind, his handsome face tanned by the sun and salt air, his voice rich and sonorous as a rollicking French melody fell from his lips.

High on a cliff he sighted Evangeline, her skirts flirting in the capricious breeze, her kerchief waving a frantic welcome.

Joyously he raised his voice and sang to her above the roar of the surf and the crashing of the waves on the crags. Then, oblivious of danger, with the impetuosity of youth, he shouted to the man at the tiller to steer straight for the shore, and as the surge of the sea brought the boat close to the rocks, he leapt from the tossing craft and climbed the cliff.

"Evangeline, my beloved!" he shouted as he reached her side and drew her into his outstretched arms. Her lissome body quivered in his embrace. Then she lifted her eyes to his and murmured, "Gabriel! you have come back!"

For an indulgent instant her lips lingered on his. Below them the waves crashed against the jutting rocks; about them the sea-gulls winged in majestic flight and, far across the Bay of Fundy the sinking sun tinted the clouds with flaming gold.

From a distance Father Felician looked on, smiled and understood. And as he walked away toward the house of Benedict he fondly recalled the swift passage of years since he had taught Evangeline and Gabriel their letters out of the same book, with the hymns and the plain-song. And how, when the daily lesson was completed, he had watched them as they hurried away to the forge of Gabriel's father to stand at the door and watch, with wondering eyes, the sparks fly and see him take in his leathern lap the hoof of a horse and, with a few deft blows of his hammer, nail the shoe into place. Smilingly he remembered how they had climbed to the nests in the rafters of the barns, seeking that wondrous stone which the swallow brings to her nest from the shore to restore the sight of her fledglings. Now they were no longer children. Gabriel was a valiant youth with a face of the morning, and she was a woman with the heart and hopes of a woman.

Now that they were together again, Gabriel and Evangeline found small need of words.

"Only three days have I been gone," he broke the romantic silence as Evangeline nestled in the shelter of his arms, "but it seemed an eternity without you. All day long the waves whispered your name, and at night the stars spelled it in twinkling letters."

He drew her closer to him. His lips swept her hair. She closed her eyes for a moment, pressing her face against his. Then she leaned back in his arms, bewitching and beguiling.

"Never have I seen you look so beautiful," he whispered, "never have I loved you more deeply."

She had waited for this moment, but

now its overpowering sweetness frightened her. In a roguish whim, not daring to trust herself further, she uplifted her nose with her forefinger and saucily taunted, "But you wouldn't love me if I looked like this, would you, Gabriel?"

Still teasing, she pushed her nose into another grotesque effect and repeated her saucy question.

Mischievously, Gabriel flattened his nose into the most ludicrous position. "Why, I'd love you, Evangeline, even if you looked like this!"

They laughed together, happy, carefree.

From the distant belfry of the rustic church in the village peeled the chimes of the angelus. The church was a symbol of the simple faith and devout lives of the Acadians. For years they had dwelt in homes of peace and contentment, with neither locks to their doors nor bars to their windows. A happy, industrious people, clinging to the quaint customs and dress of their native Normandy, their dwellings and hearts were as open as the day. The richest was poor, and the poorest lived in abundance.

As the chimes of the angelus stole softly through the pastoral peace of the village, columns of pale blue smoke, like clouds of

incense, rose from a hundred hearths, and
the toilers ceased their labors in the fields,
the shepherds returned with their flocks, and
the wains, laden with briney hay, rambled
homeward from the marshes.

Day with its burden and heat departed,
and the twilight brought back the evening
star to the sky. The air was filled with a
dreamy, magical light and the restless
heart of the ocean was consoled for a moment.

Far out on the cliff, the silvery tones of
the angelus bells were wafted to the lovers. Solemnly they faced each other with
a spiritual glow in their radiant faces, and
blessed themselves, while from the rocky
caverns below the deep-voiced neighboring
ocean crooned its benediction.

The boat from which Gabriel had swung
ashore could be seen beating along the
cliffs toward the village. It served to recall
Gabriel to the more prosaic side of his
calling.

"I must go. Francois will need me for
the unloading," he explained. Evangeline
nodded.

"But you will come to-night, with your
father?"

"Yes!—and we will let them have the

house to themselves, for René Leblanc, the notary, may be there, too!''

''Oh, they're going to discuss the marriage contract, Gabriel?''

''Of course! As though we cared for that. As long as I have you, and you have me, what else matters, Evangeline?''

''Nothing,'' she whispered.

He crushed her in his arms and then was gone. For a moment, Evangeline stood watching him as he leapt from crag to crag, and then she turned and hurried across the meadows, knowing the men would be waiting for supper.

# CHAPTER III

That evening as the stars blossomed in the infinite meadows of heaven, Evangeline lighted the candles on the mantle. In pensive, abstracted mood, she might have been a painting of the Madonna, strayed from a gilded frame, so divinely chiseled were her features in the pale yellow light.

Her father sat in his comfortable chair regarding her tenderly. He was a stalwart man of seventy winters, hearty and hale, his hair graying like a sturdy oak covered with snowflakes. Dreamily he watched the flames make smoke wreaths in the fireplace, the shadows nodding and mocking along the walls in fantastic gestures and dancing in reflected glow from the pewter plates on the sideboard.

"Why are you sad, my child?" Benedict asked, stroking her lustrous hair as she sank on her knees at his feet. "There should be nothing in your heart but joy, for tonight René Leblanc comes with your marriage contract."

26

As he spoke, tears welled up in Evangeline's eyes. "It saddens me to think of leaving you, father," she answered tremulously. "How will you get along without me?"

Benedict turned his face away with a pathetic effort to hide his own deep emotion. "I shall never be alone, my child, while I have memories of you, and of your dear mother, asleep in the churchyard."

Childlike, Evangeline crawled up into his lap and buried her head on his shoulder, saddened by her father's mention of her dead mother who had been only a tender memory for many years.

"You will not love me less, father, because I am to leave you for Gabriel?"

Benedict looked down into her troubled face and gave her a reassuring smile, trying to be gay despite the heaviness in his heart. "I shall see you every day," he exclaimed, unable to hide the quiver in his voice, "and I shall share in your happiness with Gabriel. This old place will still be home to you, little one."

Evangeline kissed him affectionately, her eyes gleaming with tears, her heart clutched with that indefinable loneliness of a motherless girl as her wedding day approaches. Surreptitiously Benedict brushed away a tear and enfolded her in his arms.

Thus they sat for some time in the flickering light of the crackling logs, musing, silent, closer to each other than they had been for many days. From the walls the painted likenesses of their Norman ancestors smiled down upon them.

Youth and old age. Youth filled with the dreams of romance; age with tender memories. Youth looking forward to future; age backward at the past. Youth with radiant face toward the sunrise; age with misty eyes toward the sunset.

The clang of the iron knocker on the door broke the tender, understanding silence. Benedict knew from the hob-nailed boots on the steps that it was Basil, the blacksmith, and by the wild beating of her heart, Evangeline knew Gabriel was with him.

"Welcome, Basil, my friend!" Benedict rose from his chair by the fire as father and son crossed the threshold. "Come, take your place by the chimney-side . . . it always seems empty without you."

The jovial face of the blacksmith, honored of all men in Grand-Pré, beamed with honest delight beneath his rugged beard at his friend's hearty welcome, and he roared out a greeting in return that set the shadows to dancing.

"My, but you are at your ease here, Benedict!" he exclaimed, glancing around and finding abundant evidence to sustain his observation, both as a man of means and a good eater.

Evangeline curtsied to him, and Basil opened wide his arms and gathered her in like a huge bear. Over his shoulder she saw Gabriel, his eyes beaming with love.

"He can wait," Basil laughed, hugging her tightly. "What a precious girl you are, Evangeline. Your father will miss you. But he has had you too long already. From now on you shall belong to both of us." He lifted her clear off the floor as though she were a babe and stood regarding her as she squirmed and teased to be put down.

"Only a few years ago I could hold you in one hand—and many is the time I've done it. And now you are a woman! Ha! Ha!" He put her down and turned to Benedict. "You would not find her like in all Normandie, I tell you. With such a daughter you are indeed a lucky man."

"And you with such a son," Benedict countered.

"Yes, Gabriel is a good boy," his father admitted. He turned and beamed upon the two lovers, shy and bashful in the presence of their fathers.

"And with such a wife," Basil glanced significantly at Gabriel, "what man could fail to appreciate his good fortune?"

From the mantle Evangeline brought two long clay pipes to Basil and her father. She filled them with tobacco and lighted them with a coal from the embers.

Another knock at the door announced René Leblanc, the respected notary, an aged man bent like a laboring oar that toils in the surf of the ocean. Over his shoulders hung shocks of silken yellow hair and astride his nose rode spectacles with heavy horn bows, giving him a look of paternal wisdom. Father of twenty children and more than one hundred grand-children, he was a figure loved and revered by all who knew him.

He greeted them warmly, although it had suited him better were the mission on which he had come concerned his own son. The night had turned cool, and he approached the fire and held out his thin hands gratefully to the blazing logs.

"Another pipe for the notary," Benedict exclaimed. It was forthcoming immediately. Evangeline's hand trembled as she lighted the pipe for René. He caught her fingers and squeezed them tenderly, and dismissed her with a smile.

Gabriel caught her eye as she came back to the table, and silently they stole from the house, leaving their elders to discuss the news of the parish before settling down to the details of the marriage settlement.

The three men smoked in silence for a time. It was René Leblanc who broke the silence.

"Has Basil spoken to you about Landray?"

"Not yet," Basil answered for himself. He turned to Benedict. "You remember that Landray who was in Grand-Pré in the Spring? He excited my suspicions with his questions even then."

"I remember him well," Benedict replied. "He was here to see me. This afternoon, Father Felician came up from the village. He told me this tale of Landray being a secret agent from Halifax. I guess nothing will come of it. We have been here these forty years since the treaty of Utrecht was signed, and I can't say we have been badly treated by the English."

"Nor I," René agreed. "But times have changed. Year after year the sloops from Boston have come nearer and nearer to our fishing grounds. There is always conflict."

"Why shouldn't there be?" Basil exclaimed hotly. "This land and its fishing grounds are ours. The Gaspereau was a wilderness until the Sieur DeRazilly came."

"True enough, my friend," Benedict agreed, "but his dreams of a New France have vanished. A few thieving free-booters, calling themselves Acadians, have given us all a bad name in Halifax and Boston. When we were poor, and the wilderness was at our very door, no one cared what happened to us. But we are prosperous now. We have made the Gaspereau bloom—and beyond question there are those in Halifax and Boston who would welcome the opportunity to burden us with taxes and curtail our lands."

"You state the case fairly, Benedict," René muttered. "We like to style ourselves Neutrals—and in truth we have no quarrel with his Majesty, the King—but in times of strife, neutrals have no rights. We are Papists, with a Protestant governor— and because we have been allowed to live unmolested for two-score years on British soil is no guarantee for the future."

"I know how you feel," Basil retorted rather sharply. "Every time we have been urged to sign this new oath of allegiance you have leaned more and more in favor

of it. You know as well as I what the oath
implies. In so many words you swear to
bear arms against the enemies of the
Crown—and that means France! I am a
neutral. I have no objection to expressing
my faithfulness to the King; but I will not
bear arms against my own people, for say
what you will, neutral or not, in our hearts
flows the blood of France, and the signing
of no paper can change the fact!"

"It is not fair to ask that of us," Benedict agreed weightily. "There are human
rights that transcend a court of law. In
the eyes of the Almighty what we have is
rightfully ours, and neither taxes nor pri-
vation shall ever rob us of it. But come, we
assembled here to-night for a pleasanter
business than this. Where are your papers,
René?"

From his capacious pockets René drew
out his parchment and inkhorn. Benedict
lighted the brazen lamp on the table, and
in quick order the signatures of Benedict
and Basil were affixed to the document,
naming the generous dower of the bride
in flocks of sheep, in cattle and in chests of
silver, fine linens, and rare laces, brought
over from Normandy in olden times and
handed down from generation to generation as precious heirlooms.

Affixing the great seal of the law to the contract, the old notary rose with dignity from the table and lifted aloft a tankard of ale and, with Basil and Benedict, drank to the happiness and welfare of Evangeline and Gabriel.

"May no shadow of sorrow fall on this house or hearth," he said solemnly as he took his leave.

"He's in a gloomy mood to-night," Basil declared as he started at the door through which René had departed.

Benedict nodded shrewdly, and there was a twinkle in his eyes.

"The reason is not hard to find," he chuckled. "Baptiste was here to-day pleading his own cause."

"So—?" Basil questioned. "I'm sorry I was so short with René."

For a few moments they sat and mused in silence. Then Benedict brought the checker board from its corner and placed it on Basil's knees. The two old friends drew up their chairs and started to play, laughing in friendly contention when a man was crowned or a break made in the king row.

At last Basil's head began to nod drowsily, and tired out with the toil of the day, he dozed as Benedict smiled and picked up the tumbling checkers. Getting to his feet,

Evangeline's father walked to the door and threw it open, looking for the truant lovers. The sinister foreboding of René Leblanc's words had not been erased from his heart, and as he stared at the sea his eyes wore a troubled look.

Far off he caught a glimpse of Gabriel and Evangeline as they wandered, hand in hand, beneath the trees.

Over the water a loon called. Quick to ward off its superstitious ill-omen, he crossed himself and raised his eyes to heaven.

"Let there be only happiness for her," he pleaded aloud.

# CHAPTER IV

## "MY LIFE I PLEDGE TO THEE—"

It grew late, but the wandering lovers
were oblivous to the passing of time. The
night was still, save for the shrill cry of
the curfews, winging over the silvery
strands of the beach. A mantle of peace lay
on the sleeping world; the Bay of Fundy,
that stretched westward until lost in the
hazy horizon, was calm; the little village
of Grand-Pré, with its picturesque coves
and fishing boats, its winding streets and
thatched roofs, had gone to rest.

Slowly they walked along a path that
rambled through the wildwood, among
fallen trees and scented bushes, until at last
they reached a woodland stream. Through
the tall branches of the murmuring pines
the moon's rays fell upon their shadowy
forms. At their feet the splashing water
gleamed with reflected light as it rushed
onward over rocks and ferns to the sea.

"Give me your hand," said Gabriel as
he stepped across the water, "and repeat

after me the words of an old love pledge, not as solemn perhaps, but more beautiful even than our marriage contract.''

Willingly Evangeline extended her hand and looked into his face, her eyes suddenly grown serious under the charm of his voice and the spell of the night.

''Over running water, my heart I give to thee. . . .''

He paused and listened. The sound of her voice came to him scarcely above a whisper.

''Over running water, my life I pledge to thee. . . .''

Tremulously she repeated the words.

''My love shall never forsake thee . . . as long as water runs.''

As the final words fell from Evangeline's lips, Gabriel leaped across the stream and caught her in close embrace. He drew forward to kiss her. She leaned back in his arms, provocative, perverse, a little afraid. Through her brain whirled the events of the night—the signing of the marriage contract, the solemn vows of love. She had given her heart, she had pledged her life, to the man she loved; and yet a strange fear lurked in her breast, sinister and startling.

A shadow of sorrow passed over her,

and before her loomed a premonition of tragedy, dark and ominous. A wild look came into her eyes. Then she heard Gabriel's voice . . . "As long as water runs." It soothed her troubled heart, dispelled doubt and misgiving and gave her a feeling of sweet reassurance. In hushed ecstasy her lips met his and lingered in a kiss, holy and spiritual.

Then he picked her up and carried her to a tree that lay half hidden in the shadows. Carefully he laid her down on the dry leaves, and she allowed him to cradle her pliant, yielding body in his arms, to caress the silken sheen of her hair, to take her hands and kiss the tapering fingers, to press the warm palms to his lips, while his eyes spoke words of love his tongue was unable to utter.

They were alone under the stars; and they were young, and life and love were before them. The world was shut out and forgotten. Why should there be any cruel gray dawn? Why could not the moonlight linger forever?

An overwhelming happiness swept over Evangeline, a joy indefinable. She threw back her head and from her full lips fell the haunting, plaintive strains of an old peasant song.

It was "L'hirondelle"—the song of the swallow, the messenger of love.

As she sang, her voice filtering away through the dark aisles of the forest, Gabriel laid his head dreamily in her lap and listened in reverent silence.

With soft, clinging fingers she caressed his hair until, lulled by the melody of her voice, he dropped into slumber. Slowly the words died in her throat and she sat for some time gazing at him with infinite wonder. Then she leaned over and kissed his unconscious lips.

How long he slept she never knew, for the moments sped away uncounted and her heart was filled with the dreams and fears of youth. The first faint streaks of pink were appearing in the eastern sky when he awakened.

"You are cold, Evangeline!" he exclaimed contritely. "Why didn't you wake me?"

"I was far too happy, Gabriel, just to have you near. As I sat here, I saw my whole life spread out before me as in a dream. And there were things I couldn't understand. It frightened me."

"Don't let any cloud mar our happiness," Gabriel pleaded. "Dreams are only dreams. As for the sea—if that was it—

I shall give it up when we are married.''

"It was not the sea, Gabriel. There were rivers, lakes and strange cities. I seemed to be looking for you—and never finding you.''

Gabriel grasped her in his arms and coaxed a smile to her lips.

"Don't let these idle musings distress you, dear. Let us live and be gay while we may. Come! Dawn is breaking. Your father will think I have not waited for the Curé's permission to take you away.''

Through the tangled path in the woods he led her out on the cliff overlooking the sea. Together they walked in silence. There was no need for speaking; it was enough to watch the spreading dawn, to see the tall spire of the village church, outlined in the vanishing darkness, and know that in the stilled street, lined with sturdy houses made with frames of oak and hemlock, such as the peasants of Normandy built in the reign of the Henries, the world still slumbered.

As they stood on the cliff, drinking in the sweet fragrance of the dawn, Evangeline saw Gabriel's eyes cloud, and she stared with him across the Basin where a small pinnace beat rapidly toward the bay.

"What is it, Gabriel?" she exclaimed.

"That is not one of our boats," he answered sternly. "I can tell by the cut of her sails. The cod are running, and these English sail in under our very noses to fish for them. It is not the first time they have done it!"

"Surely there is room for all—"

"Yes, and why then do they come here but to goad us on to some indiscretion that will bring the disfavor of the Governor down upon us? I tell you they come by design, Evangeline! Are we craven cowards, that we must accept every indignity without ever daring to draw steel in our own defense?"

"Please, Gabriel," Evangeline smiled maternally. "Don't excite yourself. I know you are brave and would brook no slight. But this is a time for prudence as well as valor."

Gabriel heaved a sigh of resignation as he turned away from the sea. "You are always right," said he. "But only fools can dare to hope that such things as this will not lead to trouble. It may be years away —and it may be to-morrow. But it must come!"

His mood chilled Evangeline, and to throw it off, she chided him good-naturedly.

"So! You scoffed at my dreams and

warned me to leave the future to itself, and yet you now pretend to fathom it and find only ill-omens.''

Gabriel had to laugh. ''Forgive me,'' he smiled.

With reluctant footsteps they left the cliff behind and crossed over the stile into the yard. She stopped at the door and took his head in her hands and kissed him lightly. When she looked up there were tears in her eyes, and she gave way to a little happy, hysterical crying.

''Good-by, Gabriel,'' she whispered.

For answer he drew her close to him, not yet ready to say farewell. The cooing of the doves finally brought home a realization of the hour.

''Go, Gabriel,'' she smiled.

He nodded, and when she had given him his last kiss, Evangeline stole into the quiet house.

Gabriel waited until he saw a light appear in her attic bedroom, and the flutter of a white handkerchief in final farewell at the window. Silently then he turned and walked back to Grand-Pré, like one in a dream.

# CHAPTER V

## "IN THE NAME OF THE KING!"

The indolent charm of a cloudless summer morning enveloped Grand-Pré as the warm rays of the sun swept over the boundless meadows, alive with grazing cattle, and glinted through the heavily-laden branches of the apple-trees in the orchards that dotted the floor of the valley. In the harbor, the sun gilded the sails of the fishing smacks that lay in the peaceful coves and turned them to gold.

Above the village, Cape Blomidon loomed lofty and sombre, its deep defiles still in shadow. Far out on the level of the dike, an ox-team tugged at a hay wain, and beside it a youth, in broad-brimmed straw hat, caught up the salt hay with his fork and pitched it upon the cart.

In the village itself the noisy weathercock, that had long since hailed the new day,. was still, but columns of smoke rose from a hundred chimney tops. Shutters were flung wide to welcome the fresh morn-

ing air, and from the clean-smelling depths
of the houses came the humming of the
looms and the sound of women's voices,
rising pleasantly above the busy whirring
of the shuttles.

Basil was at his forge, and the deep
clanging of his hammer as it bit into the
white-hot iron was echoed by the noisy
creaking of the cart wheels as the loaded
wains rumbled up and down the winding
street.

In such idyllic peace had Grand-Pré
droned through a thousand mornings, its
farmers prospering by their industry and
ingenuity, content to live aloof from the
world, untouched by the flame of conquest.

Misery and poverty were unknown. If
one suffered misfortune, it was the concern
of all. There was a neighborly kindliness
in their lives. Were it the raising of a barn,
or the building of a house, a dozen hands
were always ready to assist. And in those
sad hours, when the eyes of a loved one
were closing for the last time, it needed
only the presence of Father Felician to
assure the living that the departed had
found a safe and easy path to the favor of
the Almighty.

He was a spare little man, his hair whiter
than snow and his weatherbeaten face the

color of copper. Neither the storms of winter, the deep snows nor the angry waves of the ocean could hold him back when he came with the Host to give the last sacrament to the dying. With sublime assurance he covered the long miles through deep forests, over roads that were less than trails, making light of hunger and danger from wild beasts and marauding Indians.

For three-score years he had welcomed these Acadians at baptism, seen them blossom into manhood and womanhood only to marry them, and at last, to bid them farewell and usher them into that precious kingdom of God which was the common heritage of all.

Every day he had abundant proof of the fruit that flowered and matured in the vineyard in which he had toiled so long. The kindliness and simple honesty that he found, trooping at his heels. Young lovers Church and their deep devotion to their God was a far greater reward, he often said, than he had ever hoped to claim.

Where he walked, the children could be found, trooping at his heels. Young lovers came to him with their secrets, and found in his quick sympathy, a man as well as a priest.

This morning as he came from the church, Cleophas Villon, a boy of fifteen, ran to his side and excitedly pointed in the direction of the cove in which the fishing smacks were riding at anchor.

"That pinnace is an English boat," said Cleophas.

Father Felician was immediately interested. Even as he watched, he saw the red coats of four British soldiers.

"What misfortune comes now?" he questioned aloud. Without further ado, he strode off in the direction of the beach, but even before he reached it, the soldiers ran the yawl up on the sand, and falling into double file, marched boldly up the street, a young officer at their head.

The news of the soldiers' coming had been quickly communicated about Grand-Pré, and such men as were not in the fields drew close to hear the meaning of this expedition.

They had not long to wait. As the little troop came abreast of Father Felician, the aged priest raised his hand to interrogate the officer in charge.

"May I ask the purpose of this visit?" he inquired.

"Make way in the name of his Majesty the King!" answered the soldier.

Straight for the well in the public square the column headed. There they halted, beside the huge bell hanging over the well.

"Send for Leblanc, the notary," the officer commanded.

"I am here," René answered for himself, elbowing his way through the crowd. "What is wanted of me?"

"You are Leblanc, the notary, and *prefect* of the village of Grand-Pré?"

"I am," replied René.

"Very well! I hand you this proclamation from His Excellency, the Governor-General. Have it posted at once!"

With trembling hands René took the proclamation and unrolled it. The growing crowd pressed too close and the soldiers forced them back at the point of the bayonet. They were at the point of offering a like indignity to Father Felician when the officer stopped them.

"What does it say?" the priest asked.

"The notary will put it up on the board and all may read," the red-coat ordered.

A gasp of surprise and bitterness rose from the crowd as René fastened the notice to the bulletin board.

"Hear ye, men of Grand-Pré," the Englishman began, reading the notice aloud. "You are hereby commanded to take oath of allegiance to his Majesty, the King of England, pledging yourselves and your fortunes to the Crown in the present war with France. Sunday, a week, His Majesty's officers will be in Grand-Pré prepared to receive your oaths and enlist such able-bodied men as they may select. Signed, Lawrence, His Excellency, the Governor-General.''

The crowd groaned as they heard him out. He reached for the bell, unmindful of their disapproval, and rang it loudly. His mission fullfilled, the officer gave a command and the guard marched away to embark for Halifax. Some would have molested them, but Father Felician waved them back.

"No good can come of it," said he. "Let us not provoke violence."

For many years the huge gong hanging over the well in the public square, placed there to spread alarms among the villagers, had lain idle. But now as its huge rusty tongue, like that of a gossiping old woman eager to spread tidings of evil, wagged back and forth, it broke the peaceful tranquility of the morning. And as the raucous sound echoed far out through the valley, chilling and forbidding, a sudden wind sprang up from the southeast—a

wind which pushed before it masses of
slate-colored clouds that appeared as if by
magic from the clear horizon and cast an
ashen pall over the country-side.

Cold fear smote the hearts of the people.
Even the little children, playing in the
streets, ran whimpering to their mothers,
intuitively sensing danger lurking in the
pealing of the rusty old bell.

Quickly the housewives snatched their
little ones from the cradles and ran into the
square. Farmers in the fields threw down
their scythes or stopped their plows, and
fearful for the safety of their women-folk,
rushed toward the village, running across
fresh-planted fields and vaulting over
fences in their excited haste. Far out
across the quiet waters of the coves, the
menacing clang was heard by the fisher-
men. They abandoned the nets and boats
they were repairing and rushed to the
village.

Out in the meadow in back of her father's house, Evangeline sat with Gabriel in
the shady shelter of a towering haystack,
while he drank a mug of ale from a tankard
she had brought out to moisten the dusty
throats of the harvesters. Her slender figure in its dainty frock of pink was a
familiar and welcome sight in the fields.

She always brought a breath of freshness with her, but today she sparkled a little more radiantly than usual, for she had lingered before her mirror, knowing Gabriel would be in the fields to-day. And yet, with womanly contrariness, she had airily pretended to be surprised when he rushed out to greet her as she came plunging through the tall grasses of the sun-splashed meadow.

Startled, they both listened as the bell broke in upon their reverie. But it only tolled on and gave no answer to their wonderment.

"It may be a fire," Gabriel exclaimed, searching the sky for sign of smoke.

"No, Gabriel! That bell can mean only bad news!" Evangeline sprang to her feet and glanced up into the sky. "See how the wind blows! Look at those gray clouds!

"Clouds are often gray," he answered, and although Gabriel's heart was clutched by an indefinable fear, he laughed to hide his own alarm and gently chided her for her superstitious dread of the unknown.

"I never knew it to fail," Evangeline insisted as they ran toward a hay-cart making for the village and jumped on the back of it. "Remember the time when old Jean and Henri were killed by the bull when

they were on their way to help the La-
tours the day their third baby was born?
The same evil wind blew!''

Above the panting of his bellows, the
ominous clanging of the bell had quickly
reached Basil as he bent over his flaming
forge. Pushing his way through the excited
throng gathered in the square around the
bell, he read the proclamation and noted
with cold fear the impressive seal of the
law and the signature of the Governor-General of Nova Scotia.

An angry flush mounted his brow as he
read the announcement. His eyes blazed
and his rugged face grew distorted with
rage. Blindly he looked about for Benedict
and failed to find him.

''Where is Benedict Bellefontaine?'' he
demanded.

''We have sent for him,'' some one volunteered.

''This proclamation is a treacherous vio-
lation of our rights!'' Basil thundered on.
''We will never submit to it!''

The crowd agreed noisily with him.

By this time most of the inhabitants of
Grand-Pré had convened in the square, out
of breath from running, crowding and
pushing to get a glimpse of the proclamation. Finally Benedict came. The crowd

opened up to let him through. His mouth tightened and the cords in his neck stood out like the gnarled roots of an oak as he read on.

"We will not sign this oath," he cried, his voice making itself heard above the tumult. "We came from Europe to escape religious persecution and political oppression. We will not submit to this inhuman request."

"We stand together!" Basil shouted.

"We have built our homes here, we have reclaimed the lands from the tides with dikes built by our own hands," Benedict went on in a voice trembling with emotion. "Is it right that we give up all this for England? No! We have agreed not to bear arms against England. We will keep that promise. But England can not put guns in our hands and make us use them against our mother country."

René Leblanc shook his head as he faced Benedict.

"As I said only last night, to you and Basil, there is a purpose behind this threat. They are ready for our refusal. When we hear the alternative they will offer us— we may be glad to sign."

"Never!" stormed Basil. "When I use

a musket, it will be to defend my rights—
not to abuse them!''

With that faculty lovers have of being
able to forget everything save themselves,
the reason for their hurried visit to the
village took on less importance in the
minds of Evangeline and Gabriel almost
as soon as the mad tolling of the bell had
ceased. Perched on the back of the wain,
half-buried under the fragrant fresh-mown
hay, they were blissfully oblivious of the
excitement in the village street until the
blustering voice of Gabriel's father broke
in upon their conciousness.

''For one hundred years we have been
tossed back and forth from one country to
another without our consent,'' he was saying. ''But always we have reserved the
right not to fight against our own flesh and
blood. What right has the Governor-General of Nova Scotia to exact such a price
from us?''

''Gabriel—it *is* bad news!'' Evangeline
cried out.

With instant concern, the lovers scrambled down from the hay-cart and by sheer
force elbowed their way through the seeth-
ing, excited crowd. Swiftly their eyes
swept the proclamation. A moment later

a hand reached out and snatched the offending document from its nails and tore it into bits and threw them into the breeze with a gesture of contempt. Instinctively Evangeline clung to Gabriel, while all around them the people raised their voices in shouts of defiance to the Crown.

Across the heads of the crowd, Evangeline's eyes encountered Baptiste's. She smiled bravely at him, reading at a glance his deep concern for her in this hour of anxiety. She turned to Gabriel.

"I am afraid, Gabriel!" she murmured. "It may mean war . . . our separation . . . your death!" She trembled in his arms.

From the center of the crowd, where he had been watching the angry outburst of his people with compassionate eyes, Father Felician stepped forward. "Perhaps we misinterpret the request of the Governor-General." He raised his hand in a benign gesture for silence.

"Hear the curé!" Benedict ordered. Silence fell on the crowd.

"Let us go to Halifax and petition His Excellency," said Father Felician. His suggestion was met with murmurs and nods of approval. "Surely he will not refuse to listen to the justice of our plea."

"We will go immediately!" Evangeline heard René Leblanc declare.

"Maybe that is wise," Basil replied, "but I have no heart for such business . . . and I surmise we will accomplish nothing. However, we shall go."

Long after the crowd had begun to disperse, Evangeline clung to Gabriel, her head buried on his shouder as if to shut out the terrible vision of war and separation that flashed before her eyes and sent a shudder of fear through her slender frame.

Gabriel tried to console her.

"Don't let this distress you, Evangeline," he pleaded. "This is only a gesture to frighten us——"

"Oh, don't say that, Gabriel! You're only trying to allay my fears. You know that the trouble you foresaw is here. Only it has come sooner than you expected."

Gabriel could not deny the truth of her words. Silently he took her arm and led her away.

At the edge of the crowd, Baptiste stopped them.

"I want to congratulate you, Gabriel," said he. He offered Gabriel his hand, and the latter shook it warmly. Evangeline smiled through her tears at the two lads.

Baptiste turned to her.

"Don't be alarmed," he advised. "No matter what comes, nothing shall happen to you.

"You are right, Baptiste!" Gabriel answered with all the vigor of his youth. "Nothing shall happen to you!"

# CHAPTER VI

The port of Halifax, in the year 1755, bristled with activity for such a remote spot. Of late, Lieutenant-Colonel John Winslow, of the Army of Boston, had dropped anchor in the harbor, having with him three vessels under the command of Captains Hobbs, Osgood and Adams.

The garrison by this time having been recruited to full strength, speculation was rife among the members of the staff of Colonel Lawrence, Governor-General of the Colony, as to what impended.

Dispatching of the proclamation to the Acadians had given them a hint of what to expect, and yet it was not Colenel Lawrence's way to give notice and act later, especially in such a simple matter as forcing the French Neutrals to take unconditional oath to His Majesty.

Lawrence had the reputation of being a martinet. It was a maxim with him to act first and explain later, a course, some said that could lead to disaster in a man as ambitious as he. And there were others who saw in him the future Governor-General of all the British Colonies in the New World.

On this particular morning, as secretaries and counsellors to the Crown awaited the Governor-General, the officers of his staff stood about the door in a little group, interrogating the lieutenant who had delivered Colonel Lawrence's proclamation to the Acadians.

"Of course they didn't like it! I would have had my hands full but for their *Curé*, Father Felician. He speaks English."

"The Acadians are not supposed to be armed, but I dare say they are," a brother officer exclaimed. "They'll not submit to the new oath without a struggle. It is a bad business."

"That's what comes of being a neutral. No one is for you and every one is against you." The lieutenant won a laugh from them. "But you should see their girls," he went on. "Buxom wenches, I tell you! Eyes like midnight and lips redder than cherries."

They were urging greater details from him when the captain of the guard entered hurriedly and addressed the Governor-

General's secretary in tones loud enough
to be heard by all present.

"There is a commission arrived from the
Acadians. They are without and beg audience with His Excellency."

"Acadians?" the secretary exclaimed
haughtily. "Since when do we suffer them
to come here?"

"Then I shall tell them to leave?" the
captain of the guard inquired.

Colonel Lawrence's secretary was about
to answer in the affirmative when a fan-
fare of trumpets without warned him that
the Colonel himself was arriving.

"Have them wait," he said instead, and
waved the man out of the room.

The staff officers present drew themselves to attention, but as they awaited the
arrival of the Governor-General, questions
flew thick and fast as to the nature of the
petition the French Neutrals had evidently
come to present.

Heels clicked together then as the mas-
sive doors of the council chamber were
thrown open. A hushed and expectant
silence fell upon the room, all eyes auto-
matically focused on the doorway.

With forbidding mien, Colonel Lawrence,
strode into the room, resplendent in his
uniform of crimson and gold lace, his

sword clanking with a menacing rattle as he walked with swift, military tread. He was an impressive figure of towering stature . . . ruthless, decisive, ambitious for power and fortune.

By strange coincidence, as he arrogantly swept through the door, a white dove, basking in the sun, left its perch on top of one of the brass cannons that guarded the portal, and took hasty, frightened flight. It had a prophetic significance.

The Governor-General looked neither to left or right as he marched into the room, nor did he deign to exchange greetings with his distinguished civilian conferees who stood at rigid military attention, their countenances solemn with mingled awe and respect.

Members of his staff exchanged a furtive and knowing glance at his unusual brusqueness this morning.

Colonel Lawrence's face was set, grim and cold, as he sank into a high-backed chair, placed at the head of the council chamber directly under a portrait of His Majesty, King George II, which, with one or two paintings of military and naval battles, broke the somber grimness of the slate-colored walls.

Without comment he read the dispatches

and orders handed him by his secretary.

With an imperious gesture, he signalled the members of the council to take their seats and, eager to find favor in his cold gray eyes, they hastened to their respective places at the long shining table.

With a look of annoyance he saw that his secretary did not withdraw.

"Well, what is it?" he demanded coldly.

"I forgot to add that there is a commission of three French Neutrals, from Grand-Pré here who beg an audience with Your Excellency."

Colonel Lawrence cleared his throat angrily.

"The damned impertinence of it!" he whipped out. "Let them wait!"

The impending war between France and England was destined to resolve itself into a struggle for the possession of the American colonies, and Lawrence was soldier and statesman enough to know it. Already he had plans afoot to make his own position impregnable, and as the morning wore away and Father Felician, Basil and René Leblanc cooled their heels in the waiting-room, the Governor-General took his aides into his confidence.

Basil railed at being kept waiting hour after hour.

"If he will not see us," he exclaimed, "why does he not send us away? Are we children to sit here like this?"

Father Felician smiled patiently at him.

"It is a penance we do, I suppose. Still, we must not complain; too much depends upon the success of our mission to-day."

"You are right, Father," René agreed. "We have everything to gain and nothing to lose by waiting on the whims of this man. Being an arrogant man, he looks for arrogance in others, and finding it—vents his spleen on them with pleasure."

At last, in the council-room, the business of the day was finished. The Governor-Generals' aides and advisors arose to leave.

"Wait!" he ordered peremptorily. And then to the guard: "Bring in the petitioners!"

Again the huge double doors were flung open and the three delegates from Grand-Pré entered; Father Felician, simple yet impressive in his black robes; Basil, the blustering blacksmith, dressed in his rough clothes of gray homespun, nervously fingering his broad-trimmed hat; and René Leblanc, the dignified notary.

Their entrance was in vivid contrast to the colorful pomp and ceremony which attended the arrival of the Governor-General. But there was a certain dignity, a simplicity and firmness of purpose that marked their demeanors, which struck even the iron lord to whom they came to appeal.

Noting their humble hesitancy as they crossed the threshold into the ominous silence of the council-room, Colonel Lawrence brusquely motioned them to approach, with a quick, impatient gesture characteristic of his domineering manner.

"What brings you here, men of Grand-Pré? Is it that you come to tell me you will sign the new oath of allegiance?"

"We have come to petition Your Excellency in behalf of the Acadians," Father Felician answered. "We are a peaceable people, bound to England by the Treaty of Utrecht;" he paused a moment to lend emphasis to his words, "and to France by sacred ties of blood. I know your sense of humanity will recognize that tie and let it weigh in our favor."

The fervent simplicity of the old priest's statement was felt by the members of the council and the staff, despite an instinctive racial antagonism. Only the Governor-General remained unmoved, his eyes bridling as he heard the *Curé* out.

"So! what you really have come to tell me is that you will *not* sign this oath of allegiance!"

Father Felician shook his head patiently.

"You misunderstand me, Your Excellency," he argued. "We do not say we *will* not: we plead that we *can* not take up arms against our own people. This conflict between the land of our adoption and our mother country will be fought here in America for possession of these colonies. Wherever you find French colonists, there will you find our friends, our relatives, our very kith and kin. It can not be in your heart to ask us to make war on them— father against son; brother against brother . . ."

The eloquent eyes of Father Felician swept over the counsellors and military aides and came to rest on Colonel Lawrence. The Governor-General might have been carved of stone, for any sign he gave that the *Curé's* words had touched him.

"It is in my heart to serve the Crown!" he said at last. "I am a soldier, and as a matter of military prudence, you must sign the oath."

The Governor-General's arrogant hostility fanned the flame in Basil's breast into fire, and he burst out angrily:

"You have taken our guns and warlike weapons from us. Nothing is left the Acadian but his sledge and the scythe. What military necessity demands an oath from people already helpless?"

René and Father Felician were quick to see the disapproving glance that passed around the room.

"Perhaps we are safer unarmed in the midst of our flocks and cornfields," Father Felician hurried to say, stepping forward and trying to smooth over Basil's tactless outburst. He knew that a gentle, humble attitude was the only one with which the Acadians might hope to penetrate the cold armour of this man.

"We have no complaint against the Government," René added. "We have been fairly treated by you, Your Excellency, and by your predecessors. We have tried to repay that kindness by a loyal devotion to His Majesty, King George, the second."

His Excellency's expression remained a stony mask.

"For one hundred years our people have been handed back and forth from one country to another without our consent," Father Felician parried, tactfully overlooking the expression of enmity on the Governor-General's face. "Many of us have signed oaths of allegiance in the past, but we have reserved the right not to fight against our own countrymen.''

''And we will not fight them now!''

It was Basil who cried out, his voice thundering in the charged stillness of the great room. Defiantly he faced Colonel Lawrence, unable to restrain his emotions.

The council-room was in disorder instantly. The Governor-General sprang to his feet, a flush of anger mounting to his forehead. He started to speak, but the hot words were checked before they reached his lips, and into his eyes came a crafty cunning and the resolve to teach these Acadians a lesson, once for all.

''I should have you arrested for this impertinence,'' he said easily, his voice as casual as though he were discussing the most trivial matter of business. ''But I will be lenient—as I have always been.'' He stopped and addressed himself particularly to Father Felician. ''Go back to your people, and tell them I have taken their petition under advisement.''

He signalled that the interview was over, and slowly the *Curé* and René Leblanc led Basil away.

Within the council-room Colonel Lawrence's military aides drew up to salute.

The Governor-General answered them, and then instead of leaving, surprised them by saying:

"Gentlemen, you may retire," and his gesture included his councillors. "Colonel Winslow will remain."

# CHAPTER VII

## EMBERS OF EMPIRE

Long before the sloop in which they returned to Grand-Pré had touched shore, the news of the arrival of Father Felician René Leblanc and Gabriel had spread through the village.

Father Felician smiled as he saw the eager, shining faces and realized with what faith they relied in him to smooth the path of adversity and turn away the wrath of kings and hirelings. And yet, as the assembled Acadians saw the glum face of Basil and remarked the notary's dour expression, their hopes began to fade, and they followed the three men to the steps of the church with hushed voices.

"We have seen, His Excellency," Father Felician announced. "He was considerate enough to hear what we had to say. We stated our position fully, and though it was not to his pleasure, he promised to take our petition under advisement. He is a stern man, but, reassurred by my faith in our compassionate Saviour, in Whose hands we long have placed ourselves, I am confident that Colonel Lawrence will see the justice of our cause and be guided accordingly."

The crowd looked to the notary for approval of the Curé's words. René mounted the steps slowly and surveyed them at length before he spoke.

"Father Felician has stated the facts clearly," said he. "Lately I have been unfortunate enough to win the reputation of being a croaker—an apostle of gloom. There have been some who have gone so far as to say that I leaned toward the English. I have heard the story."

There was a murmur of disapproval from the crowd at this. Benedict Bellefontaine put it into words.

"Only fools could say such things," he exclaimed. "Your loyalty to us is as great as my own!"

"Yes!" another cried, "that is so, Benedict."

"However you interpret my conduct," René went on, "I beg you to remember that it is always wise to see both sides of a situation. I wish I might share the *Curé's* faith in some Divine intercession in our behalf in this matter, for most surely we will

have need of it. I found only hostility in
Halifax. Colonel Lawrence is no stranger
to me. He has taken our petition and promised to consider it, but I came away convinced that our plea had made no impression on him.''

René's words sobered the crowd even
more.

"It is a time for frankness," Benedict
declared. "What have you to say, Basil?"

Basil shook his head moodily.

"Nothing," he muttered. "Anything I
might say would only confirm the notary's
words. I am a simple man, not given to
scheming or taking advantage of my fellow-
men. I never learned the knack of turning
wrath away with a smile. The Governor-
General's insolence infuriated me, and I
dared, foolishly I admit, to defy him to
make us take this oath.''

"You did right!" a hothead in the crowd
shouted. There were answering cries of
approval.

Basil held up his hand for silence.

"No, my friends, it was a mistake. The
*Curé* has convinced me of that. The dove
can not fight the hawk.''

"Nor can it placate him with gifts,"
Benedict answered. "Our prosperity is
what irks these English. If we signed this

oath they would soon find other ways in which to provoke us into one indiscretion or another. We should have let the Mic-Macs wipe them out as they would have done had we not gone into their village with pleas of peace."

"Benedict!" Father Felician cried out reprovingly. "Such talk is unworthy of you." He faced them all militantly, his sharp eyes whipping them into humility. "Do you so soon forget those lessons of kindliness and patience that I have labored so long to teach you? Our tongues run away with us, and we fashion calamities out of whole cloth! Come, let us go into the church, and there, in the house of God, compose ourselves and beseech his never-failing mercy."

Silently they followed the *Curé* into the house of worship. The quiet and sanctity of the hallowed spot brought an abiding sense of peace and new-found faith to them. As things had been, so were they like to be forever, whispered the inanimate walls. Safe in the security of this familiar scene, with its mellow memories, the future took on a rosier hue, and when Father Felician began to pray, their responses were strong and fervent.

Evangeline had not accompanied her

father to town. With the *Curé* away, there
was no school, and the children, quick to
take advantage of this unlooked-for holi-
day, had tramped across the fields to Benedict's orchards, knowing Evangeline would
not send them home until their baskets
were filled with plums and pears.

For the greater part of the afternoon
she had romped through the orchards with
them. When the shadows began to grow
longer and the cows and sheep started to
move toward the barns, Evangeline led the
happy, laughing throng out upon the head-
land where she had given her heart to
Gabriel. It was a favorite story-telling
spot with the children. Each had his favorite story, and they clamored for attention as Evangeline tried to satisfy them all.

"Time to go," she warned at last.

"Oh, no, Evangeline," begged little Her-
misdas Gagnier, the chemist's son. "Tell
us about Glooskap and his pipe."

The others took up the cry and Evangeline was forced to consent.

"Very well—but this and no more. The
angelus will ring in a minute." They settled
themselves comfortably again and Evangeline waited for them to grow quiet. "Well,
when the Acadians first came to the Gas-

pereau, they didn't know that the Mic-
Macs had a great god of their own. It was
the fall of the year, and the sky was blue
with haze, just as it is to-day. We call it
Indian summer, but in those days we had
no name for it.

"Soon the Indians came to our huts to
trade. They wanted blankets. Old Father
Voisin, the Capuchin, who was here long
before Father Felician came, spoke to the
Indians and asked them why they needed
blankets; the days were still warm. The
Mic-Mac answered that soon it would be
cold, for Glooskap was smoking his pipe
up on Mount Blomindon. And when the
good Father asked them who Glooskap
might be, they told him he was the Great
Spirit, the god of the Mic-Macs.

"So ever since then, when the blue haze
hangs in the air, we call it Indian summer,
but the Mic-Macs know better. They know
that Glooskap is up on Mount Blomidon,
smoking his great pipe, and growing
sleepy. For ten days he will smoke, and
then, when his pipe goes out, Glooskap will
close his eyes. The snow birds will come
and cover him with their blankets of snowflakes. The fishes and all the underwater-
people will hunt the deep holes. The leaves

will drop from the trees; the brooks will
stop singing; ice will cover the lakes and
all the world will be still with winter.

"Through it all, Glooskap snores. Bye
and bye he stirs in his sleep, and the underwater-people call out to him to wake up and
unlock the ice. But Glooskap just keeps on
snoring. Then one day, the wild geese fly
north, looking for him. They scold and call
out, 'Wake up, Glooskap! Wake up!' But
Glooskap only sleeps sounder.

"Soon after the geese come, Teshup, the
ground-hog, pokes his head out of the snow
and looks for Glooskap. 'Wake up!' he
cries. 'Spring is here! Wake up!'

"But Glooskap sleeps on. And then one
day, when the sun smiles, Chopeesh, the
blue bird comes. In a small voice, sweet as
honey, he calls to Glooskap, 'Wake up,
wake up, wake up! S-p-r-i-n-g is here, is
here, is here!' And Glooskap sits up and
rubs his eyes. He knows that little voice.
When he moves the snows break, the ice
cracks and the underwater-people splash
and frolic. The leaves begin to peek out of
the buds; the brooks sing again; the grass
turns green—and all the world laughs, for
Spring is here."

As Evangeline had talked on she had
failed to notice the smiling face of Gabriel,

peering at her through the dark green of the hemlocks. The angelus sounded a moment later. Reluctantly the children said good-bye and wandered away toward the village.

Evangeline stood watching them. Gabriel was at her side before she discovered him.

"I was your most interested listener," he laughed as he embraced her. "I have just come from the village. My father and the others have returned from Halifax."

"And what word do they bring, Gabriel?" she asked anxiously.

"The Governor-General has agreed to consider the petition. My father is discouraged, however. He defied Colonel Lawrence to make us take up arms against France and the colonies. He says nothing will come of the trip—and the notary agrees with him. Father Felician thinks differently."

"The *Curé* would know," Evangeline insisted. "He is never wrong."

"There is a great deal to what you say," Gabriel admitted. "But enough of these calamities that are not calamities yet. I came to tell you that Father Felician will read our banns to-morrow. We will sit together in church, Evangeline."

His joy in the prospect stilled Evangeline's doubts, and hand in hand they wandered back toward the house. As they crossed the fields, she caught sight of her father, trudging homeward. His elastic step was missing, and as he walked the shoulders that usually were squared back with a wholesome joy of life sagged forward.

Evangeline stopped and called to him. He waved to them and waited as they ran to his side. Benedict put his arms around them, and three abreast they went on.

"You are worried, Father?" Evangeline questioned.

Benedict shook his head, determined to keep his fears from her. "I am disappointed," he admitted. "I wish I had gone to Halifax."

# CHAPTER VIII

### THE CROSS OF DE RAZILLY

Several days after the departure of the petitioners from Halifax, the fleet riding at anchor was augmented by the arrival of two pinnaces from Boston. Food and arms were taken on board at once. Preparations for the embarking were of such a nature that they could not well be made secret. Rumor had it that the vessels would sail on the morrow for Porte Edward—a tale that made many smile. If Porte Edward was the announced destination of an expedition of this size, it could mean only a blind to cover the real nature of the enterprise, which a select few knew was aimed at the French Neutrals. That evening three hundred foot soldiers were rowed out to the vessels.

Repeated conferences between Lieutenant-Colonel Winslow and His Excellency, Colonel Lawrence, had informed the garrison that Winslow would command this expedition. They stood together as the men embarked and then immediately returned to the Governor-General's headquarters.

Winslow's face wore none of that ardor a commanding officer is supposed to show at such moments. He paced back and forth from window to desk as Lawrence penned an order.

"What is it man?" His Excellency inquired of a sudden. "You're as gloomy as an owl."

"Truth is, sir, I have no heart for this business."

Colonel Lawrence fixed his piercing eyes on him and paused dramatically over his reply.

"But being necessary—it will be accomplished, sir! I am trusting you to carry out my orders and keep me fully advised. You will proceed to Porte Edward, as we agreed. There you will open these orders and execute them to the best of your ability."

Winslow accepted the envelope, but he refused to be thus rudely dismissed.

"You are taking a drastic step, Your Excellency—without the knowledge or authority of the Crown. On the grounds of justice and humanity I plead for these Acadians. Certainly some other way might be found that——"

"There is no other way," Lawrence cut

him off. "It is my policy to act first and
advise my Government afterwards."

"But would not a policy of consideration
for these French Neutrals be more tactful,
as well as humane, sir?"

A shade of annoyance swept over the
Governor-General's face at Winslow's
continued championing of the Acadians.

"I am a soldier, Winslow," he thundered. ". . . not a diplomat! May I remind
you that you are also a soldier?"

Winslow nodded, convinced that he but
wasted his time with this obdurate man.

"Once among these Neutrals you will
post a proclamation requiring them to attend at a certain place at a certain hour,
as you may please. Make it peremptory in
its terms—but keep its purpose vague
enough so that they may not suspect the
reason for which they are assembled. Em-
ploy fair means with them, if you will.
But if you find that such treatment will not
accomplish our purpose, you will proceed
most vigorously against them."

As Colonel Winslow saluted and withdrew, His Excellency stepped to the windows commanding the harbor and gazed at
the ships at anchor. The fire of conquest
burned in his eyes as he saw the sails
unfurl.

The tide was running, and in a few minutes the vessels began to drop away. He stood at the window until the night enveloped them. Knowing the nature of their mission, and realizing the fate to which he had consigned the Acadians, one might have expected to find some trace of sympathy or regret in his eyes at this last moment. Instead, there blossomed a complete and abiding satisfaction.

As these messengers of vengeance and a man's ambition sailed away on their long trip into the Bay of Fundy and the mouth of the Gaspereau, no hint of their coming reached the farmers of Grand-Pré.

Sunday dawned bright and clear. A pleasant warmth tinged the morning air as Gabriel waited for Evangeline on the steps of the Church. At last she came, her father driving his favorite black Norman mare. A new sense of dignity rested over her to-day, and Gabriel knowing the eyes of the parish were on them, offered her his arm with the grace of a *grand seigneur* and proudly led her to his father's pew.

Wrinkled grandmothers and young matrons, shy lovers and even the young lads still in their teens, followed them with enraptured gaze as they passed.

Father Felician entered and they rose

with bowed heads. Demure and as saintly-looking under her white Norman cap as the Madonna herself, Evangeline made her responses to the mass and stole shy glances at the lover beside her as he counted his beads.

At last the mass was over. Father Felician came out on the steps of the church, knowing Benedict had an announcement to make, and certain that to-day his parishoners would tarry to discuss the Governor-General's proclamation.

Gabriel and Evangeline were already the center of an admiring group, showering congratulations on them, and whispering advice well calculated to embarrass the bridegroom-to-be.

Gabriel smiled at the good-natured chaff of his fellows, trying to turn the barbs they levelled at him back upon the shoulders of the originators.

From a distance, Baptiste looked on, his face white with emotion. So he had once dreamed of standing with Evangeline on his arm. With choking breath he turned away to wander in the fields alone.

"*Monsieur le Curé!*" some one cautioned as Father Felician raised his hand for silence. At once the humming of voices and the jostling of the crowd ceased.

"Benedict has an announcement to make," said he.

"On Friday, weather permitting, I want you to come to my place—all of you. It will be the betrothal feast of Evangeline and Gabriel. Michael, you will come with your fiddle?"

Michael Michel, the fiddler of Grand-Pré elbowed his way to Benedict's side. His hair was as white as the *Curé's*. A pair of merry eyes danced in his nut-brown face. For forty years he had kept alive the music of their homeland, and there was never a party or feast day that was not enlivened by the gay tunes of his fiddle—a rare instrument, he always claimed, handed down to him by his grandfather who had played at the court of one of the Louies.

"Have I ever failed to be where I was needed?" Michael demanded. "Knowing the quality of your ale—what could keep me away, Benedict?"

There was a general laugh at this, for Michael's capacity for the nut-brown ale of the country-side was too well known to need comment.

"I did not ask you to come to do honor to my ale," Benedict answered with mock severity.

Again the crowd laughed, but Michael chose to grow serious.

"I but jested," said he. Turning to Evangeline he doffed his hat and bowed to the ground. "We are all proud of you, little one. I remember well the day your father brought you·to me to learn the songs of the homeland. What good times we had, you and I and Mr. Fiddle! But my little playmate has grown up. All of us who have known you so long and watched over you, share your happiness, Evangeline. If there is a tear in old Michael's eye it is only because he is so proud of you. And you, Gabriel, are a lucky boy!"

"It is just as Michael says," Esdras Prudhomme declared. "When Benedict asked me if I would take charge of the roasting pits I was cross with him. It's my privilege, I told him, and I should like to see some one else in charge."

The crowd parted to let Gabriel and Evangeline through. As they left, Benedict joined Basil.

"The young folks will prefer their own company to ours on the way home. Ride with me and let them wander over the fields as they will."

Basil nodded.

"The others are waiting," said he. "Evidently they think there may be some news from Halifax."

Even as he finished, Latour, from the marshes, a big, black-beared man, called out: "Is there anything to be learned about the proclamation?"

"No, we are still waiting to hear from His Excellency," Father Felician answered. "Every day that passes without our hearing from him adds to my assurance that all will be well yet."

The crowd broke up into little groups and stood about, chatting the news of the parish or discussing the probable decision of His Excellency, Colonel Lawrence.

Evangeline and Gabriel soon left the village behind and wandered homeward along the cliffs. They were passing the broken down cottage of the Widow Lamphrey when the old woman hobbled out to the gate and waved to them.

As long as Evangeline could remember, the Widow Lamphrey had dwelt on the cliff, her garden always a tangle of weeds and the house going from bad to worse. She had the knack of weaving marvelous baskets, and she derived more than enough for her simple needs from the sale of them.

But it was not her baskets for which the

Widow Lamphrey was best known. She had the gift of healing burns by the laying on of her hands. It was a fact that was well-known, and even the *Curé* had been compelled to admit it, attributing it to some strange manifestation of God's kindness.

It gave the Widow Lamphrey a unique position among the Acadians, and as the legend grew that she had supernatural powers, the old woman never disavowed it. Secretly she claimed to be able to read the future in one's cup.

Gabriel would have gone on, but Evangeline stopped him.

"She means well, Gabriel. Let us stop for a word with her."

"She'll want to read the tea leaves for you," he answered, unable to hide his displeasure. "Why risk being distressed on this day by what she may have to say? Certainly you do not believe that she can read the future."

"Of course not! It would only amuse me, Gabriel."

The old woman opened the gate as they approached and beamed upon Evangeline. "I have been watching for you," she cackled. "I knew the banns were to be read this morning. I wanted to hear them, but my joints are so stiff I couldn't get to mass. I guess there were plenty there."

"The Church was crowded," Evangeline told her. "Father has invited every one to the house on Friday for the betrothal feast. You must come."

"I will if I am able, but small pleasure can I take in the dances and games with my rheumatism. But there was a time, my child . . ." She paused to smile at the memories her words conjured up in her mind. "I remember the day I was betrothed to Lamphrey. He was a fine lad, then, not unlike Gabriel. Come into the house, my child. Let me read the leaves for you. They will tell you a great deal on such a day as this."

Gabriel was not pleased and he volunteered to wait outside.

"No, Gabriel, I want you to hear what she has to say," Evangeline protested prettily. "Come!"

The Widow Lamphrey led the way indoors. It was the first time Gabriel had set foot in the place, and he noted with pleasant surprise how clean the floors were, and how white and spotless were the linens.

The old woman showed Evangeline her baskets and reminisced pleasantly about her childhood as the tea steeped. Gabriel sat apart, uneasy in his mind and wishing they soon might leave.

The tea was ready at last, and as Evangeline handed the empty cup to the old woman she made strange sounds of incantation, a trick she had learned from the Indians, Gabriel whispered to himself.

Evangeline drew her chair up closer to the table and her breath came a little faster as the fortune-teller twirled the cup around and around in her hands. Then she paused and her old eyes lit up with an uncanny fire as she stared at the tea leaves. Her body grew tense and she held the cup closer to her eyes.

"What is it?" Evangeline asked nervously. "What do you see?"

The widow did not answer. Gabriel noted how the cords stood out on her long, eagle-like talons. He knew that the excitement which gripped the old woman was real to her, and as he watched he saw her deliberately squeeze the cup until it popped out of her hands and fell upon the floor in a dozen pieces.

"One of my good cups, too," she groaned. "What clumsy fingers"

Her attempt to make the dropping of the cup appear an accident chilled Gabriel's blood and to avoid Evangeline's eyes, he bent down to pick up the shattered bits of china.

The feeling that the old woman had seen something in the cup that she did not want to tell her, gripped Evangeline, and she questioned her about it.

"Was there something there that frightened you?" she asked, her face whiter than she knew.

The Widow Lamphrey only shook her head. "No, my child," she murmured. "All I saw was a journey—you and Gabriel."

"Well, that is nothing to grow excited about," Gabriel declared, trying to calm Evangeline and get her away.

"Of course not," the old woman agreed, wondering how much he had seen.

They started to leave. Widow Lamphrey called Evangeline back.

"Wait," she said as she rummaged in a drawer. "I have something that I have saved for you Evangeline. Let it be my wedding present." From the drawer she drew a small crucifix attached to a thin silver chain.

"It was blessed by the Pope," she explained. "It once belonged to the Sieur De Razilly. Its charms are great. Wear it always, Evangeline; it will bring you luck and guard you from danger."

"The Sieur De Razilly once owned it!" Evangeline exclaimed as she gazed at the cross with reverent awe. "I—I shall always wear it," she murmured.

The Widow Lamphrey watched them go. They were out of sight of her house before Evangeline voiced the thoughts that were troubling her.

"Wasn't it strange, Gabriel, her dropping the cup? And telling me I was going on a journey! Don't you remember that the night the marriage contract was signed I told you I too dreamed that I was going on a journey—only you were not with me. I was searching for you. . . ."

"You see?" he chided her. "You said she would only amuse you, and yet you believed every word she said, and now you are troubled with vague misgivings when we should be alive with happiness and laughter."

He was sorry immediately for his quick words as he saw Evangeline's lips quiver. He took her into his arms and fondled her tenderly.

"I am silly, I know," she breathed softly. "But if I should lose you, Gabriel!

Where you go, I must go. Promise me you will never leave me.''

He lifted the cross of De Razilly.

''On this crucifix I swear that no act of mine shall ever part us!''

Back in her cottage the Widow Lamphrey rocked disconsolately.

''I couldn't tell her,'' she moaned.

# CHAPTER IX

## THE BETROTHAL FEAST

Under the open sky Benedict Bellefontaine spread the betrothal feast of
Evangeline and Gabriel. From long rows
of barbecue pits arose the savory odors of
roasting meats—great halves of beeves,
whole baby lambs, pigs and turkeys—growing tender and juicy over the glowing
coals.

Esdras Prudhomme was in his glory.

He was a pompous, jovial man, given to
expostulations and wild gesticulations when
his culinary authority was in danger of
being encroached upon. He walked along
the pits, testing and turning the meats and
glancing with good-natured suspicion out
of the corner of his eye at three hungry
boys peering from behind a tree, ready to
pounce upon them with his menacing fork
if they but made a false move in the direction of his treasured viands.

Benedict was in a gay mood, the worries
of the past days put aside. Early in the

morning guests from all the country-side
had begun to arrive, some walking, some
riding in wains cushioned with hay and
drawn by lumbering oxen, and some on the
broad backs of Norman horses. Before the
sun reached its zenith, the rambling house
and spacious yard were alive with happy
throngs, children at play, men chatting
over their mugs of foaming ale, quaintly
dressed maids and matrons fluttering from
place to place, a blaze of color in their
kirtles of blue and scarlet.

Into the yard rambled a huge farm horse,
across whose broad back six small children
were straddled, their arms firmly entwined
round one another, laughing in childish
delight. Suddenly the small tot on the
horse's rump lost his balance and, without
warning, slipped down the tail of the animal, dragging the other children after him
in a tumbled heap upon the ground.

Anxious mothers ran toward them, but
they were up and away with a shout of
laughter.

From under the spreading branches of
the sycamore tree, Gabriel, who, with Basil,
Benedict and Father Felician greeted the
guests as they arrived, looked off and saw
the mishap, amused at one curly-haired
little youngster, his chubby face covered

with dust, who had not yet decided whether
the fall was a joke or a tragedy. Glancing
back, the child caught Gabriel's eyes upon
him and, anxious not to appear to disad-
vantage in the sight of Gabriel, he grinned
and scrambled away in pursuit of the
others.

Beyond the porch, on a rustic bench built
around the trunk of a tree, René Leblanc
beamed as he sat surrounded by his one
hundred and twenty-five grandchildren, all
waiting anxiously and impatiently for their
turn to listen to the mysterious tick-tock of
his great watch, a rare possession in those
days. As long as there was a child to listen,
René was happy, for he never tired of
watching the astonished expressions on
their chubby faces change to pleased wonderment as he held the watch to their ears.

In the seclusion of her attic bedroom,
Evangeline, radiant with happiness, had
dressed for the festival in a snow-white
lace-trimmed cap, a kirtle of pink that was
rivaled only by the excited flush of her
cheeks. With modest pride she displayed
the treasures of her wedding chest to a
coterie of eager-eyed young maidens from
whose lips escaped gasps of admiration
and ecstasy as their gaze lingered long-
ingly on the fine linens, embroideries and

demure frocks of blue and pink and lav-
ender, with their filmy collars and cuffs of
old Norman lace.

"This one came all the way from
France," Evangeline exclaimed, and drap-
ing over her shoulder the most elaborate
frock in her trousseau, she gaily pirouetted
about the room, vivacious as of old, her
coquettish movements, followed by the
sparkling, adoring glances of the girls.

As they gazed at her enraptured, the
mischievous black eyes of one of the girls
wandered from Evangeline and focused on
something half hidden away in a corner of
the hope chest. Quickly, with a sly, unseen
gesture, she pulled out a pair of tiny
knitted boots. Then with good-natured
deviltry, she beckoned to the other girls,
dangling the little baby boots before their
eyes.

"From Grandmother Laroque," Evangeline protested.

Tittering and choked giggles answered
Evangeline. A look of horrified embarrassment came over her face, and laughing to
hide her confusion, she snatched the little
boots away, cuddled them tenderly against
her cheek for a moment and tucked them
away, shaking her finger in reproach at

the teasing girls who thoroughly enjoyed
her blushing discomfort.

"Your trousseau is lovely, Evangeline."
The mischievous one, whose prying curi-
osity had started the trouble, took mercy
on Evangeline and changed the conversation. "But don't keep us waiting. Show us
your wedding gown!"

Evangeline knelt before the chest and,
flushing with pride, tenderly lifted out her
beautiful wedding gown of shimmering
white silk, trimmed with flounces of cob-
webby lace caught up with great ribbon
bows . . . a creation of exquisite fineness
and lustre such as never before had been
seen in Grand-Pré.

"It is fit to grace the court of a King!"
Azalma of the black eyes exclaimed.

With stately dignity Evangeline held its
soft, caressing folds against her lissome
body and, parading up and down the room,
gave a demure impression of how she
would walk down the aisle of the church
to take the marriage vows with Gabriel.

Azalma had cast her own eyes at Gabriel,
and there was an unwitting echo of it in
her voice as she exclaimed: "I envy you,
Evangeline!"

Entranced, the girls looked on with

dreamy, worshipping eyes, each unconsciously picturing herself going to the altar
to marry the man she loved and dreaming
of her own betrothal feast when she too
would proudly display the treasures of her
wedding chest.

Beside the huge oaken doors of the living-room, Gabriel and a restless group of
young men waited for the girls to come
downstairs. They called out for them to
hurry at last. Finally the patter of feet
rewarded them and they glanced up and
caught sight of dainty black slippers and
shapely ankles, flashing beneath lace-edged
petticoats as the girls, led by Evangeline,
trooped down the stairs. No sooner had the
girls appeared, than a pair of arms en-
circled the waist of each and carried them
off in search of old Michael, the fiddler.

"You are yourself again," Gabriel found
opportunity to whisper.

"I am happy to-day!" Evangeline answered.

On a bench at the south side of the
house, hard by the cider-press and beehives, old Michael smoked his pipe, smiling contentedly at the happiness around
him, his jovial face aglow like burning
coals when the ashes are blown from the
embers, the slanting shadows of the trees

overhead playing on his snow-white hair as it waved in the breeze.

"Play for us, Michael," the young men cried.

"Play for you?" he ruefully repeated their question, as Evangeline and the girls danced around him, begging for music. "But how can I call the figures of the dance when my throat is parched?" With twinkling eyes he looked suggestively down at an empty tankard at his side.

"We'll remedy that!" Azalma exclaimed.

As if inspired by a single thought, the girls darted off toward the old ale-house. They were back presently, and Michael found himself confronted with a semi-circle of smiling faces beaming at him above a dozen tankards of foamy ale.

"Now will you play, Michael?" they demanded.

Smacking his lips with gusto, he drained one of the mugs, and ordered the others placed beside him. Then he picked up his fiddle and drew the bow across the strings in a lively dance, his wooden shoes beating time to the music as the strains of *Tous les Bourgeois de Chartres* filled the air.

Soon the dance was in full sway. To Evangeline and Gabriel was awarded the

place of honor. Gallantly, he bowed to
Evangeline as she sank into a deep curtsy,
radiant and willowy. The music moved
faster and faster. Young and old lined up
in a great circle and looked on with smiling faces as the dancers merrily whirled
in the intricacies of the different steps as
Michael called out each movement.

From the shady security of a tree, Baptiste looked on, his heart heavy, his dreamy
eyes following Evangeline as she flashed
sly, flirtatious glances at Gabriel, joining
hands with him at last and making an
arbor under which the other dancers
passed with light tripping steps.

Baptiste was about to turn away when,
Evangeline, dancing back and forth in time
to the lively music, chanced to catch a
glimpse of him, half hidden behind the
tree. With a smile of deep understanding
she ran over to him and drew him into the
circle beside her, forcing him to enter into
the gay spirit of the dance.

"You shall be my partner, Baptiste,"
she cried gaily, placing his arm about her.

With no jealous pang in his heart, affectionately understanding her generous gesture, Gabriel quickly turned to Azalma and
catching her round the waist, led her into
the circle of dancers.

"Such happiness!" Basil exclaimed feelingly. "So we should always be were we let to our own devices."

"Let us not give way to gloomy forebodings on this day," Benedict gently reproved him. "We are still free men."

Father Felician agreed heartily with Benedict. "I have never seen Evangeline in gayer mood. This is her day, and let us not cast a shadow on it."

So, unaware of impending disaster, the merrymakers danced on, faster and faster, with carefree abandon, as innocent and natural as children at play, while into the peaceful stretches of the Gaspereau silently sailed the Governor-General's ships of war on their mission of vengeance, and even the Widow Lamphrey, hobbling about on her cane in the shade of Benedict's trees, had no premonition of their arrival.

"Long life and happiness to Evangeline and Gabriel!" Basil's lusty voice rang out as the guests gathered for the feast at the long tables spread beside barbecue pits.

Father Felician raised his hand in a blessing.

"Long life and happiness!" the crowd echoed his words and lifted high their tankards of ale.

"Long life and happiness to Evangeline

and Gabriel!'' Baptiste shouted, though the words choked in his throat as he faced Evangeline, standing in the shelter of Gabriel's loving arms, the happiness of her heart revealed in the tender expression of her eyes as she looked up into her lover's face, bent over hers in ardent admiration.

"Eat your fill!" Benedict urged his guests. "There is plenty for all."

Esdras and his assistants moved along the tables, trying to serve them in order, but they were hard-pressed in their task, for everywhere they turned a phalanx of empty plates greeted them.

"Let us sing the songs of the homeland!" Benedict shouted above the din of voices as his guests congratulated the betrothed and proposed toast after toast.

A shout of approval greeted Benedict's suggestion.

"*Le Carillon de Dunkerque* it shall be!" Michael cried, and his fiddle broke into a tuneful melody and the feasters took up the song of the betrothal. Their voices ringing out in resonant unison, echoed through the orchard and floated out to the crags and caverns of the sea, to mingle and be lost in the surge of the tide.

Song followed song, and as Michael

swept them along with his music, their voices grew louder and louder. They beat on the table with empty tankards, keeping time to the rhythm of the song.

Evangeline sang with the others, all her misgivings and gloomy forebodings forgotten in this hour of happiness.

Suddenly the swell of voices was stilled as the martial beat of drums penetrated the air.

"What can it mean?" Evangeline gasped. Gabriel caught her and they faced the drums together, as the startled guests drew back, bewildered and speechless.

"The troops have come!" Basil shouted. Over the stile and into Benedict's yard marched a column of British soldiers.

With measured tread they came on, their guns bright in the sunlight, their coats red as a blood-stain.

"So it was for this that we waited!" Basil cried in bitter denunciation. "Fools that we were, not to accept the warning they gave us! Instead of preparing, we've wasted our time in prayer and pleading!"

Father Felician's eyes blazed as Basil's hot words fell on the air. He drew himself up militantly. "Say no more!" he cried. "Are you mad, that you mock the power of the Almighty? Perhaps some friendly mission brings these soldiers among us.''

The *Curé* glanced at Benedict for confirmation of his words, but Benedict sat with bowed head, as Evangeline and Gabriel hovered over him.

# CHAPTER X

## "FATHER, FORGIVE THEM!"

"Hear ye, men of Grand-Pré!" The cold, official tones of the burly English captain fell upon the ears of the amazed Acadians with ominous solemnity.

"You are commanded by order of the Governor-General to assemble at once in the church of the village."

The crowd muttered its disapproval. Men put their women-folks behind them and faced the armed soldiers without flinching.

A wave of fear swept over the face of Evangeline. Instinctively she clung closer to Gabriel, in this moment of impending danger. Angry protests fell from the lips of Basil and Benedict as they made their way through the crowd to the commanding-officer.

"You have no right to intrude, sir." Benedict cried, his eyes blazing with indignation. "This is my daughter's betrothal feast."

"This is a sacred right with us," René Leblanc began. "I beg you . . ."

"Will you come or shall I be obliged to use force?" the captain demanded sharply. "You will gain nothing by offering resistance. In the village, Colonel Winslow and three companies of infantry await your presence."

News that such a force had been dispatched to Grand-Pré staggered them.

Father Felician was first to regain his composure. In his benign way, with uplifted hand, he turned to his parishoners with a reassuring smile.

"Let us obey, my people," he pleaded fervently. "In the house of God we have nothing to fear."

To this many agreed, and the few who refused and started to leave were brought back at the point of the bayonet.

"I shall not be parted from you!" Gabriel muttered savagely as he held Evangeline to him.

"Fall in!" a soldier commanded. He placed a hand on the boy's shoulder. Gabriel was about to knock it away when Evangeline stopped him.

"I will follow you to the church," said she. "Go! lest they run you through."

He kissed her again, as the soldier smirked at them, and ran a keen, appraising eye over Evangeline.

Gabriel could see his father, Benedict, and even the *Curé,* waiting for the word to march.

In quick, military precision the red-coated soldiers pressed the men into line and marched them away. Anxiously the frightened women, their whimpering children tugging at their skirts, followed the long, sad procession.

Evangeline passed the Widow Lamphrey.

"It was this you saw in my cup," Evangeline told her.

The Widow shook her head. "You are mistaken, my child," and for once the old crone spoke the truth.

As the Acadians entered the village, they saw soldiers everywhere, and in the harbor, riding at anchor, their guns trained on the town, the three men-of-war that had brought them.

Straight to the steps of the church the detail of soldiers marched the Acadians. Between columns of flashing bayonets they entered the holy place.

The sacred atmosphere of the rustic house of worship took on a grim, military aspect as the armed soldiers reached their places and stood at rigid attention around the walls, in front of the windows and before the altar, with its shining crucifix of silver aind its gold candlesticks, their muskets casting grim, menacing shadows across the gleaming whiteness of the lace altar-cloth.

"It's a trap," Basil warned his son in low whispers as Colonel Winslow, tall, erect and soldierly, entered from the chancel, nervously fingering the Governor-General's proclamation as he waited for the Acadians to sink into the pews.

"Men of Grand-Pré, you are convened here this day by order of His Excellency, Colonel Lawrence, Governor-General of Nova Scotia, to hear his answer to your petition," Winslow began reluctantly, his attitude evidence enough that the task before him was a painful one.

A great silence settled upon the church, broken only by the uneasy scuffing of the soldiery as they stood at attention. Winslow paused to study the parchment document he held in his hands.

"His Excellency desires to recall to you the fact that for more than forty years the Crown has shown you greater consideration and leniency than has been the indulgence of its subjects in any part of its dominions.

"You have been called upon many times

to take this oath of allegiance to this Government. Always, as in the present instance, you have sought to claim the rights of neutrals, refusing to take up arms against the enemies of the Crown or pledge yourselves and fortunes to its success.

"Now, therefore, it is the final resolution of His Excellency that, grievous as the consequences may be to you, and disagreeable as my task is to me, you be informed that as a penalty for your refusal to agree to take up arms against the enemies of the Crown and pledge yourselves, fortunes and goods, if necessary, to the proper prosecution of the war with France, all your lands, cattle and such livestock as you may possess are forfeited to the Crown, together with your dwellings and such harvested crops or stores of wheat and other grains as are in your granaries, and that they are now and henceforth the property of His Majesty, King George, the second."

As the dreadful import of his words slowly made its way into the consciousness of the assembled Acadians a groan of bitter anguish, not unlike the bending of a tree under the lashing of a storm, arose from their lips and was echoed by the wailing of the women without.

Colonel Winslow raised his hand for silence. The words came slowly to his lips, and it was with an obvious effort that he steeled himself before he could go on.

"Your household effects and such cash monies as you possess, are, by the special permission of His Excellency, to remain your property. Further, it is the especial and peremptory command of the Crown that you and all of the French inhabitants of Grand-Pré and the several villages of the countryside be removed from this Province now and forever and be conveyed to the colonies of New England, Maryland and Carolinas. God grant that you may dwell there ever as faithful subjects—a happy and peaceable people! I therefore declare you prisoners in the name of the Crown!"

A portentous silence followed his words. Too stunned for speech, the Acadians sat and stared dumbly at the King's officer.

"Transports for your removal will arrive in a day or two. I respectfully request you to remember that accommodations will limit the extent of such household goods as you may take with you, being mindful of the fact that I desire whole families to go in the same vessel, you will gauge yourselves accordingly."

Slowly the speechless wonder that gripped his listeners gave way to a rising wail of rage and anguish. Louder and louder it grew, and the soldiers lining the walls shifted about, their guns ready. Suddenly the storm broke, like the angry waters of a released torrent that sweeps everything before it in its mad, bellowing plunge down a chasm, so the Acadians rose in billowing waves.

"Down with the Governor-General? Down with all tyrants!" shouted Gabriel.

"Death to those who would rob us of our homes and farms!" cried Basil, his eyes wild with baffled rage.

Their voices rose in angry volume. Gabriel's defiant outburst firing them into open rebellion. Springing from their seats they rushed madly for the doors and windows.

"*Vive la liberte!*" Gabriel yelled above the din of their angry cries. They took it up.

"*Vive la liberte!*"

"*Vive la liberte!*"

The soldiers guarding the doors lowered their bayonets.

"Run them through if they advance another step," a sergeant shouted.

It had the desired effect on the others,

but Gabriel flung himself at the bristling line of bayonets as though they were not there. A blow from the butt of a musket felled him.

Outside the church, Evangeline beat her hands against the oaken doors and cried out: "Gabriel! Gabriel!"—and got no answer. Basil heard her cry, and like an angry bull set himself for the charge, when into the midst of the angry chaos, Father Felician entered from the chancel. He paused beneath a painting of the crucifixion and raised his hand with a solemn gesture.

Colonel Winslow fell back before his gaze. The soldiers also sensed his power.

"What is this you do, my children? What madness has seized you?" cried he. He faced them, his arms outspread. "Here, where the crucified Christ gazes at you from His cross, you give way to rage and hearts overflowing with hatred."

"Would you profane the house of God with your violence?" His gentle, compassionate eyes searched the bewildered faces of his parishoners.

The soldiers fell back and slowly the tumult of angry voices was stilled and the men of Grand-Pré sank into their seats.

"Forty years of my life I have labored among you and taught you, in word and in deed, to love one another. Is this, then, the fruit of my labors and privations and prayers?"

His eyes, darkened with rebuke, fastened on his flock. "Have you so soon forgotten all those lessons of love and forgiveness?"

Turning, Father Felician met the eyes of Colonel Winslow.

"Our children have been baptised here . . . our people married. Out in the churchyard repose the remains of our loved ones. It is a sacrilege to turn this place of worship into a military prison!" The old priest's voice trembled and his eyes flashed with holy wrath.

"It is a military necessity," Colonel Winslow replied, wincing at the rebuke. The *Curé* pointed dramatically to the huge crucifix of Christ that hung on the wall. The Acadians, now wholly under his quieting influence, followed his gaze and stared transfixed at the cross.

"My children," said he, "in this hour when the wicked assail us, let us repeat the words of the Master and say, "O, Father, forgive them! They know not what they do!"

Reverently he bowed his silvery head, and crossing himself, addressed his plea to God.

His compassionate words fell like a benediction on the vast assemblage, now prisoners in their own church. With sobs of contrition, they sank to their knees, bowed their heads and murmured, "O, Father, forgive them!"

# CHAPTER XI

"YOU ARE MY LIFE!"

As darkness began to fall, the guards came out and told the waiting women and children that the men would remain in the church over night and ordered them to disperse to their homes.

In their grief and misery they turned to Evangeline, and forgetful of self, she sought to cheer them with words and demeanor, hoping to show them by her meekness and patience that she had not given up hope.

Urged by their household cares and the weary feet of their children, they began to move away across the fields and down the winding street.

From the steeple, as though nothing were amiss, sounded the angelus. It brought a hint of peace to Evangeline, and she stole away into the dusk of the churchyard, listening for some sound from within the walls that held her father and lover.

The guard had changed and half a dozen

soldiers lounged along the wall after her,
casting knowing glances in her direction
and exchanging bawdy comments among
themselves concerning her. Colonel Winslow stepped out and took in the scene at
a glance.

"Go home, my child," he said to Evangeline, his voice husky with the strain of
the day's business.

When she had left, he summoned the
captain of the guard. "Establish sentry
posts at once," he ordered. "No one will
leave the church-yard without leave from
me."

Shortly after the expedition pitched its
tents beside the church.

Evangeline wandered home as the stars
began to blossom. Across the fields came
the plaintive lowing of the untended kine,
their udders heavy with milk.

Like one in a dream she wandered past
the tables spread for the betrothal feast.
Coals still glowed in the pits. When the
cows had been milked, she returned to the
silent house, her steps weary and slow.

In the kitchen she found honey and
cheese, brought fresh from the dairy that
morning, but she could not eat. Disconsolately she lighted the the hearth and
stood beside her father's favorite chair

dazed and bewildered by the sudden change
of events that had ruthlessly swept away
the happiness of her betrothal festival.
She drew the great armchair in front of
the fireplace at last and slipped down into
its depths, pondering deeply over what
fate held in store for her and Gabriel, de-
pressed by the haunting loneliness of the
silent house in the eerie stillness of the
night, and imagining in the rustling of the
withered leaves outside the window that
she heard the sound of stealthy footsteps.

Staring into the dying embers of the fire,
her beautiful face spiritual in its poignant
sadness and her troubled eyes mirroring
the anguish and suffering of her heart, she
presented a somber figure, hardly recog-
nizable as the gay, vivacious Evangeline
who had only a few short hours before
exhibited the treasures of her wedding
chest to the maidens of the village and
danced with Gabriel to the merry strains
of old Michael's fiddle.

With echoing steps she mounted the
stairs to her bed-room. Long after midnight she awakened to hear the driving
rain beating down on the withered leaves
beneath the sycamore. The lightning flashed
and the answering thunder boomed across
the sky.

In some indefinable way this evidence that God was still in His heaven brought a sense of peace to Evangeline.

But in the church in Grand-Pré, lighted only by the fitful gleam of the tapers on the altar, the soldiers stationed at the huge doors refused to listen to the imprisoned men who clamored for the privilege of visiting their loved ones. The first thought of the stricken men had been for their families.

At last the guards sent for Colonel Winslow. Basil and Benedict approached him with their request and he at once granted the release of twenty men, holding the others as hostages to insure their return.

Immediately all surged forward, anxious to be among the chosen few. Gabriel struggled with the others and finally made his way to Colonel Winslow and pleaded to be selected as one of the favored twenty. His heart sank as he saw the officer shake his head.

"You are too late," snapped Winslow. "The last man has been selected."

Benedict Bellefontaine, scrawling his trembling signature on the list of the chosen ones, looked up and caught the tragedy in Gabriel's face, saw him turn and walk away, his eyes heavy with disappointment and despair. With a quick stroke of the quill Benedict crossed his name from the parchment list and wrote Gabriel's name in its place.

"Let him go in my stead," Benedict pleaded with Colonel Winslow. "He is my daughter's betrothed."

The old man's trembling lips, the tears in his voice and his willingness to deny himself, moved the stolid officer to sympathy, and he acquiesced to the substitution of lover for father.

Gabriel started to protest.

"She would have it so," Benedict answered simply.

Joyously Gabriel accepted the generous offer. His heart was young and his desire to see Evangeline was all-consuming.

"Tell her to be brave," Benedict murmured.

With quavering lips and moistened eyes, he saw Gabriel led to the door with the others who were to leave. Unsteadily, his head reeling dizzily in the stifling air of the crowded church, Benedict made his way back to a seat near Basil and Baptiste.

Surprised, Basil glanced up from his seat

**as** Benedict slowly sank down beside him.
"Benedict! I thought I heard your name
called as one of those to be released!"

"It was called, Basil, but I let Gabriel
go in my place!" Benedict's voice was list-
less, his eyes blurred with tears of weak-
ness and exhaustion. He was like a mighty
oak suddenly stricken by lightning, so deep
had their unhappy fate plunged its knife
into his heart.

Basil could not answer. A great lump
came into his throat as he realized the full
significance of the man's sacrifice. Gruffly
he reached out and put an arm around
Benedict's shoulder with the understanding affection of two old friends, brought
closer together by their children's love for
one another.

Baptiste's face lighted up as he heard of
Benedict's sacrifice for Gabriel. He found
it in his unselfish heart to be grateful that
Evangeline was to be granted the comfort
of Gabriel's presence in these tragic hours
of sorrow and uncertainty that had engulfed them all.

Like one possessed, Gabriel dashed
through the rain. The storm passed before
he reached Benedict's house.

His imperative knock aroused Evangeline from her racing, troubled dreams.

Trembling, hand hesitant on the latch, her heart beating with fear, she called out.

Gabriel's reassuring voice reached her ears and her nervous fingers quickly released the bolt.

"Gabriel!" she cried.

"We are all prisoners in the church," he explained breathlessly as he enfolded her in his strong arms. "Only twenty have been released . . . the others are held to guarantee our return."

She snuggled up to him, a sweet reassurance creeping over her as she listened to Gabriel's story of her father's sacrifice.

"Surely they will let me see him to-morrow."

"I hope so," he replied without conviction, dreading the moment when he would have to tell her the truth. He walked over to the fireplace and kicked the graying embers into flame. Tremulously she followed him, peering anxiously into his troubled face and overwhelming him with a flood of questions.

"Tell me the truth," she pleaded.

Gabriel bowed his head, knowing she must be told.

"Our lands—our cattle—even our homes have been taken from us!" he finally answered, the words falling from his lips like a deadly calm on a gloomy sea. "We are to be deported! Driven into exile . . . scattered from Boston to New Orleans! Everything is lost, Evangeline . . . everything!"

She drew back, a gasp of horror on her pallid lips, her mind in a dizzy whirl, unable to grasp the terrible import of his words.

"No, Gabriel," she cried hysterically, "not that!"

"So it has been ordered. The ships to carry us away will arrive to-morrow or the following day."

"And you will go on a journey . . . Evangeline muttered the words to herself more than to Gabriel. "She knew—and I knew! It is as I dreamed, Gabriel!"

"We will not wait for them to send us away," he answered quickly. "The forest is close. We can steal away before morning. The Indians will hide us. . . ."

"No, Gabriel, we can not leave our fathers. They are old; our place is with them."

"You are right," Gabriel admitted. "They will need us more than ever now." He drew her into his arms, his heart aching as he tried to console her, smiling to hide his own anxiety and fear. Unable to control her pent-up emotions, Evangeline cried without restraint, shaking with convulsive sobs, engulfed in the dark, forbidding waves of the great catastrophe that had befallen them.

"The tyrants!" he groaned out bitterly. "God forgive them!"

"Gabriel, my beloved," Evangeline whispered after the first shock of the tragedy had spent its force, her eyes brave through her tears, "they may take our lands . . . drive us from our homes," she choked back her tears as the words trembled on her lips, "but nothing shall ever separate us . . . nothing shall take from our hearts the great love God has given us!"

"Colonel Winslow has promised that whole families shall go in the same boat," he exclaimed, her courageous words bringing a new flame of hope to Gabriel.

"All is not lost, beloved," she whispered bravely, "for if we love one another, no harm can come to us, whatever may happen!"

"You are my life!" he cried. His face lightened as he smiled back at her and saw shining in the depths of her dark eyes, fringed with their tear-laden lashes, the beauty and strength of a woman's devotion . . . affection that hopes and endures and is patient.

"Out of the ruins of our dreams, Evangeline," he told her, and his voice was vibrant with resolution and promise, "in the unknown land of our exile, we shall find the realization of our love!"

They looked long at one another, each trying to console the other, while out of the debris of their youthful hopes rose a new-found happiness, a love strengthened by the tragedy they faced together.

# CHAPTER XII

## "WHERE ARE YOU, GABRIEL?"

It soon became apparent to Colonel Winsolw that he would need the assistance of the men imprisoned in the church in the matter of impounding the livestock and collecting the herds and driving them to the village.

Accordingly, he appeared before them at once. They had not slept throughout the night, and they stared at him with red-rimmed eyes.

"Something may have happened to our advantage," René Leblanc whispered to Benedict.

Benedict gave no heed to his words.

"Men of Grand-Pré," Colonel Winslow addressed them. "It has become apparent to me that my soldiers can not accomplish the bringing together of your cattle and livestock without your assistance. If you will take oath to make no attempt to escape nor to hurt, kill or destroy anything of any kind, whether it be crops, livestock or what not, you will be allowed to depart from the church with the distinct understanding that you are to report here for the night, before sundown.''

Bitter as was this reprieve from their prison, the men gladly accepted Colonel Winslow's conditions. The church doors were opened and they were free to go.

Father Felician stopped them for a moment.

''Take advantage of this opportunity to instruct your women in the matter of the household goods we are to take with us,'' said he. ''It would save confusion if they were to begin to assemble them on the beach.''

So the day passed, with the Neutrals doing the bidding of their masters. The huge wains, heavily laden with goods began to move toward the beach. Tagging along, beside their mothers and elder brothers and sisters, the children clasped their playthings in their tiny hands, intent that they should not be left behind.

On the beach itself, great piles of goods began to grow, seemingly in hopeless confusion, and yet, the owners knew where every article was placed, and to guard them were prepared to spend the night on the sands.

Father Felician moved about among them, cheering them on with his kindly words and admonitions.

From the fields and pastures the men brought the livestock, their eyes hot with smoldering resentment as they turned over to the soldiers the fruits of their toil.

Benedict had found Evangeline waiting for him. Her heart smote her as she beheld him. The glow was gone from his cheeks, and his eyes, that had always danced with a merry light, were heavy and dull. Even his footsteps seemed weighted with the sorrow in his heart.

"We are to collect the cattle and grain," he said simply. "You will collect such goods as you care to take from the house."

He sank into his chair and sat without moving, like one in a trance, as he stared through the open window at the broad fields that his industry had claimed from the ocean.

At noon, their own simple tasks completed, his farm-hands came to assist him.

Evangeline urged food on him, but he refused it and walked away with the men.

In that house of many heirlooms and things rich with the memories of childhood, Evangeline knew not where to turn in her desire to take everything with her. The wain her father had sent was filled at last, and she started away for the village, only to stop a dozen times as she remembered some treasured possession that could not be left behind.

Half way to the beach she encountered Gabriel.

"The transports have arrived," he told her. "We should have taken to the woods as I suggested. Many have, and when the roll is called to-night they will be found missing."

Gabriel spoke the truth, and when the prisoners lined up at sunset, and Colonel Winslow discovered how many were gone, he stormed in righteous indignation.

"It is thus that you repay me for my kindness," said he, and his face grew sterner than they previously had seen it. "The transports have arrived. Therefore you will spend the night here and embark in the morning."

In brooding silence they heard him out, secretly wishing that they too might have taken to the long dim trails of the forest.

No bright star of hope rose for them that night. Basil and René sat with Benedict and planned that they should go on the same boat, that in some new land they might gather about them the friends and companions of their youth.

Gabriel sat apart with Baptiste.

"If I am separated from her, promise me you will protect her with your life, Baptiste, Gabriel urged.

"I swear it!" answered Baptiste. "But Colonel Winslow has promised that we shall not be separated."

"I know—but I am in disfavor with him. He suspects that it was I who urged François and the others to flee. If he gets proof of it, I'll be punished.

The night wore away at last. In the cold, penetrating fog of early dawn, the men were told to get ready to leave.

"The young men will go first," an officer shouted.

"We do not want to be separated from our fathers," Gabriel protested.

The officer brushed him aside. "The young will march now. Go!"

Sons and fathers clasped hands and embraced each other, fearful of what this move might mean.

Gabriel said farewell to Basil and reluctantly started to follow the others. A soldier pushed him back.

"You will remain," said the officer.

Soon the men were made ready. An order was barked at them and they filed out of the little church with measured steps. Only Gabriel was left.

Colonel Winslow approached him presently.

"I have definite proof that you aided and abetted the escape of the prisoners yesterday," said he. "Your young men evidently look on you as their leader. That you may realize the folly of your conduct and recognize the futility of further inciting them to disobedience, the town shall be fired, and you will be made to witness the burning."

"You tyrants! You fiends!" Gabriel screamed as they led him away.

The human herd, destined for exile in alien lands, poured down to the cold bleak shore of the Gaspereau in the silence of desperation, pausing ever and anon to glance back for one last glimpse at the homes of their childhood with all of their precious memories.

Around fitful fires of driftwood, the women and children huddled in forlorn groups, the sound of their cries of anguish and woe mingling with the monotonous moan of the sea as they waited their turn to be crowded into dories and rowed out through the beating surf to the transports riding at anchor, dark and sinister in the ghostly gray light.

Under guard came the young men. Mothers called out to sons; sisters ran forward to embrace their brothers.

Evangeline leapt forward with the others, looking for Gabriel. Baptiste saw her.

"Gabriel was held back," he informed her. "He asked me to tell you to wait."

The men of Grand-Pré followed almost immediately. The guards were not able to keep them in line as wives and mothers and children greeted the heads of their families.

Colonel Winslow waited for the confusion to subside. Half an hour passed without bringing order. The masters of the ships sent word that they must be ready with the tide. It galvanized the Colonel into action.

Father Felician was leading his people in prayer. "Let us sing 'Sacred Heart of the Saviour,' " he called. They responded bravely.

Winslow waited until they finished. Then

without ado gave the order for the embark-
ation to begin.

Knowing there was no time to lose, the
soldiers hurried the exiles into the dories.

The tumult grew. Despite Winslow's
orders, families were parted, wives were
torn from their husbands, mothers and
fathers separated from their children.
Everywhere the pitiful cries of those who
had lost sight of their loved ones rent the
air, rising above the roaring of the surf as
it pounded out its dirge of doom.

"Mama! Mama! I want my Mama!"
rose the heart-rending cry of a little girl
whose chubby arms were outstretched to
a dory tossing in the surf. It reached the
ears of Baptiste as he walked along the
shore searching everywhere for his father.
Without hesitating for a second, he picked
the little tot up into his arms, and as the
boat carrying the frantic screaming
mother out to sea was borne toward the
shore momentarily on the crest of a wave,
he tossed the child through the spray into
the safety of its mother's arms.

Colonel Winslow had himself rowed out
to his flagship, unable to further witness
the scene taking place on the shore. Once
abroad, he stood in the shadow of the
bridge, overseeing the deportation, hasten-

ing the unloading of the people as they reached the transport and were led down into the hold of the vessel. He winced as he saw the rebellious few felled with a gun butt for refusing to obey orders.

In the cold gray mist, Father Felician, forgetful of self, went from group to group, cheering the people of his parish in their hour of tragedy, comforting them as best he could and blaming their plight on his own failure to reach the ear of God.

"Our Father in Heaven," he prayed as another forlorn group, making ready to embark, gathered around him asking for spiritual guidance and blessing, "fill our hearts this day with strength and submission and patience. Weak though we are, do not desert us."

Wandering with faltering footsteps from fire to fire, old Michael, dazed and pitiful, played disjointed snatches of melodies, hoping to lighten the burden of his people. A burly soldier grabbed the fiddle from his hands suddenly and crushed it into the sand with the heavy heel of his boot.

"Get into the boat!" he growled.

Under the shelter of a rocky ledge, waiting for Gabriel with ever-growing concern, Evangeline turned from searching the crowd to administer to her father, a terrible fear clutching at her heart when he did not answer her words of endearment but gazed at the flickering light of their campfire with glassy eyes. His expressionless face, haggard and worn, without thought or emotion, was like the dial of a clock from which the hands have been removed.

"Father," she pleaded, "don't give way. For my sake. . . ."

Benedict tried to muster a smile for her, but it died on his lips. "I'll be all right," said he. "Find Gabriel."

She left her father's side and darted away to peer into the faces of another group of prisoners. Gabriel was not among them.

"There can not be many more to come," she said to Esdras Prudhomme.

"We are the last," Esdras answered.

Father Felician approached hurriedly.

"Everything is arranged for your going abroad," said he. "As a special consideration the families of Leblanc, Lajeunesse and Bellefontaine will go together."

"But Gabriel—he is not here," she cried in fresh dismay. "I've looked everywhere for him. We can not go without him, Father!"

"Didn't he come with the young men?"

"No! I couldn't have missed him," she moaned, her eyes unceasingly scanning the faces of those passing by. With a sob of despair, she turned away from the *Curé* and ran down the sands crying, "Gabriel! Gabriel! Where are you?"

# CHAPTER XIII

### FAREWELL TO ACADIE

Alone in the deserted church Gabriel waited. He rattled the doors, but they were still locked. At last a ruffian shouted: "Attend, Gabriel Lajeunesse!" The door was thrown open and Gabriel marched out into the empty street.

Half a dozen soldiers were running from house to house, touching their torches to the thatched roofs.

Gabriel started to hurl himself at one of them when a bayonet was pushed against his back. None of that, my bucko!" a coarse voice boomed in his ear.

With bloodshot eyes Gabriel saw his own home offered to the flames.

"We'll teach you Frenchies a lesson!" a soldier mocked him.

"And you call yourselves men!" Gabriel dared to taunt him.

The soldier swung at him. Gabriel dodged away and let drive with his own fist. The man went down and lay still. The sergeant in charge came running.

"Turn around!" he cried, and as Gabriel faced about they hurried him away, prodding him with their bayonets and hoping he might try to break away.

Father Felician had tried to follow Evangeline, and now as she came back to Benedict, the *Curé* caught up with her.

"He is not here," she wailed.

Father Felician was about to answer when his old eyes caught sight of the flames rising from the village.

"They are burning our homes," Benedict moaned. "It is the final blow."

Suddenly the bleak morning was luridly lighted and the misery of the huddled groups on the shore was brought into sharp relief—mothers cradling crying babies in their arms, the old and the sick grouped together in crumbled heaps of hopelessness, lovers clinging to each other in frenzied fear of separation, little children clutching their broken toys. Rising piteously above the clamor sounded the frantic barking of dogs, racing from group to group in search of their masters.

"God have mercy!" mumbled the *Curé*.

From a hundred housetops flames leaped high as the homes of the Acadians were given to the torch. Columns of smoke rose as the wind seized the burning thatch and

whirled it through the air. Frightened by
the fiery whirlwinds billowing about them,
the bellowing herds and horses broke from
their fences and folds and dashed madly
over the meadows in thundering stampede,
the work of yesterday destroyed in a
twinkling.

Higher and higher leaped the flames,
gleaming on land and sea and mocking the
tragic plight of the exiles. Aroused from
his stupor by the brilliant glare, Benedict
Bellefontaine tried to rise to his feet to
catch the last glimpse of his burning home.
Feebly he sank back in a trembling heap.

"We shall never see our home again, my
child," he muttered incoherently, "nor our
beautiful land of Acadie!"

"Fiends out of hell!" a voice roared. It
was Basil, terrible to behold in his rage.

Vainly Evangeline tried to keep back the
tears that filled her eyes as she saw the
happy home of her childhood consumed.
She smothered a cry of misery as she vis-
ualized the hungry flames, perhaps at that
very moment, eating their way into her
treasure chest and greedily turning to lifeless gray ashes the filmy lace and shimmering silk of her wedding dress.

Farther up the hill, nestling against the

grassy slope, was the thatched-roof cottage to which Gabriel was to have taken her as his bride. As a column of black smoke rose from its roof and engulfed the cherished spot where they had spent so many precious hours planning and dreaming, she hid her tear-stained face against her father's shoulder to shut out the vision and cast from her heart the stark fear that perhaps she might never see Gabriel again.

But suddenly into her troubled eyes leapt a gleam of tragic joy as she beheld her lover, walking between the soldiers. She sprang to her feet and ran to him, all her morbid fears dispelled in the protection of his arms.

The soldiers tried to force her back.

"We have been waiting for you, Gabriel . . . so long," she murmured breathlessly. "Now I shall get Father. Let nothing separate us!" she warned as she darted away. "We are to go together!"

She was at Benedict's side immediately.

"Come, Father! Gabriel is here!" Feverishly she tried to make him understand. With Father Felician's aid she helped him to his feet. Bravely Benedict tried to walk, but slowly his determination gave way, his

legs tottered, his head fell on his chest and
with a choking gasp he pitched forward
on the wet sand.

"Father! Father!" Evangeline screamed, a cold terror seized her. Benedict did
not answer, and a wild, half-crazed look
came into her eyes as she gazed at her
father's ashen face and realized that the
pall of death was upon him. "Speak to
me!" she implored. But Benedict's head
sagged forward on her breast. Slowly she
raised her eyes and searched the *Curé's*.

"He . . . is . . . dying!" said Father
Felician as he bowed his head and prayed.

"He . . . is . . . dying!" muttered the
crazed girl.

"He . . . is . . . dying!" echoed the
mournful waves of the surging sea.

The soldiers had hurried Gabriel along,
intent on showing him no consideration
whatever for his attack on their compan-
ion.

From the jutting crags where the sailors
were crowding the men and their families
into the dories, Gabriel looked back and
saw Evangeline fall prostrate across the
body of her father, sobbing and kissing
his cold, lifeless face.

"Let me go!" he shouted defiantly as he

tried to break away. The soldiers closed in on him, but Gabriel fought back desperately, determined not to give in, finding in his arms the superhuman strength that often comes to man and animal alike when they are trapped.

He slipped and went down. A boot-heel flashed out and ripped his scalp. With a strange little groan he fell on the sand unconscious, the blood gushing from his head and staining his face.

Evangeline, already hysterical with grief, lifted her tear-drenched eyes just in time to see the soldiers pick up Gabriel and ruthlessly pitch him into a tossing dory.

Frantic, not knowing what she was doing, she sprang to her feet and dashed to the water's edge as the sailors struck out for one of the transports. She stared at the receding dory, and saw Basil bend over and pick up Gabriel.

"Gabriel! . . . Gabriel! . . . come back!" she screamed.

She saw Basil argue with the sailors. They pushed him back into his seat and went on.

At her wits' end, not knowing which way to turn, torn between her love for

Gabriel and her duty to her dying father, she plunged into the sea and waded out waist-deep into the pounding surf.

"Gabriel ... my Gabriel!" she called piteously, her eyes wild with terror. The sound of the sea drowned her voice, but her delirious lips continued to call out the name of her lover.

Fearful lest she be carried out in the fierce undertow, Father Felician waded in after her and half carried her drooping form back to the beach.

"You must not fail me," said he. "You must be the inspiration of us all."

On board the crowded transport, in the confusion of the milling, wailing throngs frantically crowding the rail for a last look at their homeland, Gabriel regained conciousness. Awakening to the terrible realization of what had happened, he evaded the guards and made his way into the rigging, determined to leap into the turbulent sea and battle his way back to Evangeline.

"Nothing shall keep us apart!" he groaned. He was about to leap when suddenly the strong hands of his father pinioned his arms through the shrouds and held him helpless and struggling.

"Don't be mad, my son!" Basil pleaded.

"Father, let me go!" Gabriel cried angrily, no longer himself in his anxiety. Furiously he tried to fight free. "I must go to Evangeline!"

"You know I would be the last one to hold you back, my son . . . but this is folly. In this mad sea you would never make the shore. It is suicide to try it." He patted Gabriel's shoulder sympathetically and wiped the blood from his cheeks. "Take heart, Gabriel . . . Evangeline and Benedict may come out in the next dory!"

For a moment Gabriel was consoled. Then he glanced up and saw the crew going aloft to unfurl the sails. A moment later he felt the vessel lurch as she weighed anchor and swung around. The tide caught her and she began to move away even before the wind filled her sails.

"We're leaving!" Gabriel shouted. "The ship is sailing!"

Basil nodded his head but only held him tighter.

"Let me go! Let me go!"

Basil's eyes filled with sympathetic tears at his son's grief, but he did not loosen the vise-like grip in which he held him, determined not to allow him to jump to his death in his hysterical frenzy.

As Evangeline stared out to sea, her eyes riveted on the transport that was carrying Gabriel away, she saw the sails flatten out in the wind.

An unintelligible groan broke from her lips. Her knees gave way and she fell convulsively over the lifeless body of her father, her hair disheveled, her wet clothes clinging to her slender body, her face grown old in her tragic hour of despair.

"He . . . is . . . dead!" said the priest.

"He . . . is . . . dead!" moaned the girl.

"He . . . is . . . dead!" mocked the sea.

## CHAPTER XIV

The days of that October were bleak.
Ever beating to the southward, the vessels
that bore the Acadians sailed at last into
the harbor of Boston, their provisions exhausted, their water unfit for drinking and
sickness taking its daily toll.

The designs and ambitions of the Governor-General of Nova Scotia found small
approval in Boston Town when it became
apparent that the Commonwealth must
bear the expense of supplying food and
medicines to the French Neutrals.

While the Council argued and dispatched letters to Colonel Lawrence, some
of the Acadians were landed, to wander
through the Commonwealth, vainly seeking homes and employment. In due time,
some food and medicines being forthcoming, the vessels sailed away with the unhappy exiles, distributing them in the
ports from Maryland to the Carolinas.

Speaking an alien tongue and bound together by the bonds of a common misfor-

tune, the Acadians clung together, seeking their kith and kin, guided by hope or hearsay. Friendless, homeless and needy they wandered across the mountains to the headwaters of the Ohio.

Urged by a restless longing, ever searching for Gabriel, Evangeline wandered with them, often in want and discomfort, but cheered by Father Felician, her friend and confessor.

"Somewhere I must find him," she often said.

"We shall go on until you do," he always encouraged her.

And yet, when months had rounded out into years and no word came from Gabriel, she often sat beside some nameless grave and wondered if it might be the grave of her lover, and longed to slumber beside him.

In a fur-post on the banks of the wide Ohio, a *coureur-des-bois* by the name of Ledoux gladdened her heart with the news that he had seen Gabriel.

"His father was with him," said Ledoux. "It was at the mouth of the Wabash that I met him. They were headed for Louisiana."

Evangeline pressed him for the details of that meeting.

"It *was* Gabriel!" she exclaimed. "He lives!"

"Of course," Father Felician agreed. "So I have always told you.

The following day they took passage on a *batteau* bound down the river. It was a crude, unwieldy craft, manned by Acadian boatmen. They sang as they poled or rowed, and the songs they sang were the *chansons* of her homeland.

"Again I see you smile," Father Felician said happily. "God is kind."

Past the mouth of the Wabash, where Ledoux had met Gabriel, and into the brown flood of the Father of Waters the boat glided. The days grew warmer. The grass turned green again, the air warm and fragrant with the perfume of magnolias. At last they drifted into the tropical bayous of Louisiana, where dwells perpetual summer.

From a boatman on the river they learned that there was a colony of Acadians on the Bayou Têche.

Slowly, through myriads of water lilies and lotus, the cumbersome barge made its way into the Têche. The waters grew sluggish. Overhead the towering cypress met in mid-air, their branches festooned with trailing garlands of Spanish moss, hanging so low in places that they touched the rippling surface of the water.

The moon rose, round and resplendent, turning the dark caverns beneath the cypress and live oaks into bowers of silver where the herons waded.

Sustained by a vision that beckoned her on, and the knowledge that through these waterways Gabriel had wandered before her, that every stroke of the oars was bringing her nearer and nearer, Evangeline stood in the prow of the boat and peered into the shadowy distance.

Like a tenuous network, narrow channels led away into the darkness. The boatmen hesitated once or twice, but at last agreed on the channel they were to take.

"Sound the bugle!" one of the oarsmen urged. "Let us not pass Gabriel during the night!"

The steersman lifted his horn and blew a blast that awakened the echoes and sent them reverberating away through the leafy aisles of the forest.

At last, Evangeline slept, but the boatmen rowed on, and when they broke into song, she smiled in her sleep, dreaming it was the voice of Gabriel.

Before noon of the following day, they emerged from the shadowy caverns of the trees. There before them, basking in the sun, lay the Atchafalaya.

They glided past numberless islands where the Wachita willows bent low over the banks with their shade. As afternoon wore away, Evangeline was aroused by the distant strains of familiar music. She listened intently, and faintly to her sensitive ears came the indistinct, dream-like strains of an Acadian song.

The boatmen caught her excitement and bent their backs with redoubled effort. The *batteau* leaped ahead, and soon, clear and distinct came the lilting strains of *Tous les Bourgeois de Chartres.*

With heart beating wildly, Evangeline turned to Father Felician.

"It is the song of Acadie!" she cried. Her voice trembled with joyous excitement. "Some of our people are near! Perhaps . . . at last . . . I shall find Gabriel!" Her troubled face, grown spiritual with the weary, empty years, lighted with a new, sublime hope as she listened, clutching the arm of the faithful old priest, who shared her excitement.

"It is Saint Martin!" sang the boatmen, knowing their journey was at an end.

Five years had passed since the first Acadian exiles had come to Bayou Têche.

They had built houses of logs and taken up anew their struggle with the forest, clearing land and putting it to seed.

The fertile savannas in this rich land of Attakapas rewarded them handsomely. From the resident French in New Orleans they had received only kindness and hospitality.

After the long years of travail and wandering, this welcome was almost more than they could bear. In their hearts they knew they had come home. Not only had the Government welcomed them, but had given them ploughs and the nucleus of the herd that already had multiplied into abundance.

In this land of plenty, the ploughshares cut through the black loam as easily as the *pirogue* slipped through the water. It was always summer. No need here to prepare for the long hard winters they had known.

Always a thrifty people, they had prospered in this new land of opportunity. The soft French of Louisiana was not unlike their own. It brought them friendships and understanding.

Wild animals—the red deer and the antelope—abounded on the wide prairies of Opelousas. Game was everywhere, turkeys and pheasants and ducks and wild fowl beyond number. No where else in the world were the waters so rich in their treasures.

It was a land to warm the heart of hunter and trapper, and the farmer, released from the drudgery of winter, fought the rising waters of Springtime with a smile, knowing they but made his land more fertile.

Only the fever had they to fear. The charms and cures for it were many, and they soon learned how to combat or avoid it.

René Leblanc, the notary of Grand-Pré, lived among them, and his letters had gradually drawn other wandering Acadians to the banks of the Têche. His eyes had grown misty with age in the years that had intervened, but the fibre of the man was apparently as tough and sturdy as ever, and as he saw Baptiste prosper in this new Acadie, the days of suffering were forgotten.

Baptiste had not married. His father knew why, and wondered if ever his son would erase from his heart his love for Evangeline. They had often spoken of it. René had pointed out more than one dark-eyed beauty who would have brought credit and comfort to Baptiste, but his answer was always the same: "In my heart there is room for only one."

They were the very words Evangeline

had spoken to him when she refused him. Baptiste had not forgotten.

Five years to the day had passed since the Acadians had come to the Teche, and they were gathered together this afternoon to celebrate their coming with a feast of thanksgiving.

As the *batteau* neared the shore, Evangeline could hardly contain herself. Even placid Father Felician felt his blood pounding through this gnarled veins.

Under a blossoming oleander she saw a musician. He was bent over his fiddle and was vigorously pulling his bow back and forth across the strings, nodding and smiling to the throng of maidens and young men who curtsied and bowed in time to his music.

Evangeline stared spellbound for a moment.

"It's Michael!" she cried gaily, her voice carrying across the water to the group on shore.

The dancers stopped at her glad cry and Michael stared back at her in dumb amazement. He fussed with his glasses and finally recognized her.

"It's Evangeline!" he called. "Evangeline Bellefontaine!"

He threw down his fiddle and ran to the

water's edge, his old joints as spry as ever.

From a distance Baptiste had heard him call Evangeline's name. Sure that it was only a trick that his ears had played him, he did not quicken his step as he neared his father, idly amusing himself as of old with a group of children, clamoring to hear the mysterious tick-tock of his treasured watch.

Baptiste watched the dancers running to the shore, old Michael waving his arms excitedly. He followed them with his eyes. Baptiste saw her then. He brushed his hand across his face, expecting the vision to vanish. But she did not disappear. Just in back of her he recognized Father Felician.

A cry of joy fought its way to his lips, and with a mad rush he ran toward her, calling her name and bidding her welcome.

Evangeline threw her arms about him, carried away with happiness at being back among her own people again.

"We looked everywhere for you," Baptiste declared. "My father wrote many letters asking about you. No one seemed to know. But I always said you would find us."

Evangeline smiled at him in his joy at seeing her.

He was still slender and handsome. As she studied him and let her eyes rest on his, she knew that Baptist loved her as much as he had that August afternoon when he came to ask her to be his wife.

With a pang she remembered his many favors in the dark days of their expulsion from Acadie, his unfailing loyalty and never-flagging love, and she stood there, her lips mute, impatient for news of Gabriel, yet dreading to see Baptiste wince at her question.

Michael and the others dropped to their knees as Father Felician stepped ashore and raised his hand in solemn benediction. Baptiste could only stand and stare at Evangeline.

Finally the words tumbled from her lips.

"Gabriel . . . where is Gabriel?"

Baptiste's throat tightened and he caught his breath. He knew she had not changed, that she would never change. The old words came back to him—"In my heart there is room for only one."

He bowed his head resignedly. Back in Grand-Pré she had been only a girl. She was a woman now, more mature and accordingly less likely to be swayed by anything he might say. The passing years had left their mark on her. She was still beautiful beyond compare, but a new and strange spirituality lay upon her face instead of the sparkling fire he had so often surprised there.

For a moment he was afraid to speak.

"He is not here, Baptiste?" Evangeline gasped, thinking he was only trying to keep something back from her.

With a heart-breaking gasp she saw Baptiste slowly shake his head. Like a stricken doe that stands at bay before the gun of the hunter, she waited for him to speak.

"Gabriel is not here. Three years ago I saw him in New Orleans."

"Three years ago!" Evangeline whispered. "I was there—but he had gone. He was looking for me, Baptiste?"

"Everywhere—even as I! I once heard that he had journeyd to St. Louis to deal in furs."

"I was there, but Gabriel had gone."

René had hurried down to greet the arrivals, and after a word of hearty welcome to Father Felician, he turned to embrace Evangeline, knowing it was for her that his son always had waited. A second glance at Baptiste warned him that already his son's hopes had been dashed to the ground.

"It's a pleasure to see you, Evangeline!'' he told her. ''And our good Father Felician! We shall build him a church and he will find a new flock here along the bayous. Soon we shall all be united again. Where have you been these many years?''

''Searching for Gabriel,'' answered Evangeline.

''Searching for Gabriel,'' René repeated. ''And he is not here!''

''But we will go on until we find him,'' Father Felician comforted her.

''What Gabriel is this?'' questioned a squat little man who only lately had come to the Têche.

''Gabriel Lajeunesse, the son of Basil, the blacksmith,'' said Father Felician.

''I know them both,'' the man declared with an air of great importance. ''Basil is rich. He lives on his ranch far to the north-west among the Osages. Gabriel was there with him, only a month ago, but tired with some restless longing, and unable to abide the quiet existence of life on the ranch, was preparing to go to the west, to become a *coureur-des-bois*, trapping beaver and otter.''

''This is good news—and doubly welcome to us in our disappointment at not finding him here,'' the old priest declared as he urged the man for a detailed description of the way to Basil's ranch.

"It will take you several weeks," said the man.

"No matter how long it takes—we shall go!" Evangeline told him.

"But first you shall rest and join in our feasting," Baptiste pleaded. "There's so much that we have to tell you."

"We won't let them leave until to-morrow," Michael declared with a great pretense of authority. He picked up his fiddle and a lively tune broke the tenseness of the moment. Evangeline smiled wanly, understanding and appreciating his sympathetic endeavor to lighten the burden of her heart.

"We shall stay until to-morrow," she nodded.

# CHAPTER XV

A shout of gladness broke from the crowd at Evangeline's decision. Michael's fiddle sang louder than ever. The dancers caught his purpose at once, and, intent on cheering her drooping spirits, dragged Evangeline into the circle with them.

She protested prettily, but they would not take no for an answer.

As they reached their places in the line, men opposite maidens, Baptiste gently led Evangeline to the head of the column . . . the same position she had taken with Gabriel when they danced at their betrothal festival, then light of heart and radiant with happiness.

"Are you too weary?" Baptiste smiled at her.

"No, Baptiste," she replied, hoping to please him.

The dancers swayed gracefully toward one another, and the dance began with a gay swishing of lace-edged petticoats, the rhythmic patter of tapping feet, keeping

time with the music. With a valiant effort,
Evangeline smiled at Baptiste and sank in
a deep curtsy.

The music began to move faster. She felt
her head whirl, and she leaned heavily on
Baptiste's arm.

A few steps more and she swayed dizzily.
With a stifled cry her slender body
crumpled in a swoon and she fell in a pitiful little heap at the dancer's feet.

"Evangeline!" Baptiste cried. "She has
fainted!"

Instantly he was kneeling at her side.

Picking her up gently he carried her into
his home, murmuring into her ears words
of love and affection he would not have
dared had she been able to hear.

The day that Evangeline promised to
linger at Saint Martin lengthened into a
week before she was strong enough to
undertake the long voyage through the
bayous and up the Red River in search of
Gabriel.

"We must leave to-morrow," she told
René, beset with dark doubts and misgivings that while she lingered there Gabriel
might be leaving for the untracked fast-
nesses of the West.

But standing in the doorway at sunset,
gazing out across the broad bayou, she

wondered vaguely if she was not following a phantom lover, or else why she had found Baptiste and not Gabriel?

As she stood at the door, musing quietly, a hand reached out and clasped hers. Startled from her dreamy reverie, she turned and faced Baptiste.

"It is so restful and peaceful here, Baptiste," she murmured.

Baptiste did not release her hand.

"Why not remain here with us forever?" he pleaded. Unburdening his heavy heart with the words he could no longer hold back, he drew closer to her. "I have prospered, Evangeline. I can give you a home. I can make you happy."

With quivering voice he pleaded his unselfish love and waited for her to reply.

Evangeline's lips trembled, but she could find no words with which to answer. Slowly she withdrew her hand. Not wanting to hurt him, she walked away, finding seclusion under a moss-hung cypress tree at the brink of the bayou.

But Baptiste was at her side, hovering over her.

"I have never loved any one but you, and I have never ceased to hope, Evangeline. . . ."

Again she turned and faced Baptiste, who, mistaking her kindness for indecision, rushed on with growing confidence. Under his ardent gaze and the spell of his voice, Evangeline wavered. The emptiness of her fruitless years of search rushed back to her . . . the suffering and hardship . . . the uncertainty and the pain of heart.

In a daze, she suffered Baptiste to caress her hand, to kiss the tips of her fingers, to pour out his intense love for her. Then her glance fell upon the rippling water, and there came back to her the scene of her love pledge with Gabriel. The solemn words of that promise rang in her ears. "My love shall never forsake thee . . . as long as water runs."

What matter though she searched forever . . . and did not find him? Still she would go on . . . even to the end.

The still, placid bayou began to ripple in romantic fancy at her feet, gurgling, splashing . . . "as long as water runs."

"I shall never marry another," he urged.

"I am sorry, Baptiste," she whispered, so low he barely heard, and looking up into his eyes continued, "but when the heart is empty, the lips are dry."

Baptiste understood the significance of her words and dropped his head in silent acceptance.

"I shall never speak of this again," he groaned.

"Whither my heart has gone, my hand must follow . . . try to understand, Baptiste," Evangeline pleaded kindly, through misty tears.

Disconsolately, Baptiste sank to the ground, and sat with bowed head. For a wistful moment Evangeline looked at him. Then she knelt at his side and stroked his hair, a tugging pity in her heart that she could not return the great love he felt for her.

The rising moon, streaming through the rustling branches of the willows, cast its mellow rays on them, pathetically lonely and heartbroken, unable to console one another in this hour of tragic grief.

That evening Michael and the others came to say farewell.

"Come back to us soon," Michael begged.

"We shall not be gone long," Father Felician encouraged him.

In the morning, while the sun was still low in the east, they rowed away across the Têche.

"Farewell, Baptiste!" Evangeline called back across the water.

"Farewell!" came his quavering answer.

In the course of the day she and Father Felician left Baptiste and the friends of their homeland far behind. Day after day they glided over the waters of the bayou and up the mighty Mississippi and into the Red River, their *pirogue* like the shade of a cloud on the prairie, the splash of their oars awakening legions of water-fowl and breaking the deep quiet of the wilderness.

"We move so slowly," she murmured protestingly. "Is the current so strong?"

"Be patient, my child," Father Felician comforted her in her loneliness. "Silence and sorrow are strong . . . but patient endurance is God-like. Let me hear you sing. Give us *a la claire fontaine!*"

Revived by his simple, kindly words, Evangeline threw back her head and the melody of the old love-song fell from her lips.

"There is a note of happiness in your voice to-day, my child," Father Felician remarked.

"I *am* happy, Father," Evangeline answered. "Something in my heart tells me that Gabriel is near."

"Child, thy words are not idle," answered the priest with a smile of sweet reassurance. "Trust to thy heart and have patience. It may be true that Gabriel is near for we may not be far from the home of Basil!"

Nearer and near as Evangeline sang, picking its swift way among the islets that studded the river, came a light canoe, paddled by a youth whose face was thoughtful and careworn. His hair, still black as midnight, fringed his face with its neglected locks.

His look was older than his years, in his eyes the restless gleam of the wanderer who seeks in vain for the fabric of his dreams.

From afar, he heard the ephemeral sound of Evangeline's voice. Like a dog who springs to attention as it first scents the stag in its flight, so this youth leaped to his feet in the frail canoe and stood listening, his senses strained and attentive.

It was Gabriel, wearied of life, on his way to the fur country to seek oblivion in the mountains and wilds of the forest.

Nearer and nearer came the two boats, bearing the searching lovers closer together.

"I can sing no longer," Evangeline faltered, overcome with poignant memories of Gabriel. The melody died in her throat and she clung to Father Felician. "My thought of Gabriel was but a foolish dream. . . ."

Breathlessly Gabriel drifted and listened, and failing to hear the singing again, sank back and picked up his paddle, dismissing the thought from his mind as a cruel trick of fancy.

"And I heard her so plainly," he mused sadly.

Silently and swiftly his canoe glided along under the lee of an island and passed . . . passed within a stone's throw, behind a screen of palmettos, the heavy *pirogue* that carried Evangeline and the *Curé* of Grand-Pré, the heart of each crying out with longing for the other even as the sound of their paddles died away in the distance. . . .

# CHAPTER XVI

### "WELCOME, MY FRIENDS!"

On the banks of the river, half hidden in a grove of red cedars, that blocked the march of the limitless prairies that swelled away to the horizon, stood the home of Basil Lajeunesse, the blacksmith of Grand-Pré, blacksmith no longer but the lord of a landed estate as large as half of Nova Scotia.

Large and low was the ranch-house of comfortable Spanish architecture. Climbing roses wreathed the wide veranda that half circled the house. Silence reigned over it, broken only by the cooing of the doves and the song of whip-poor-wills as evening came on apace.

Above the chimney a lazy column of blue smoke rose into the sky. From the direction of the prairie came the sharp hoof beats of a cavalcade of galloping horses. A little cloud of dust traveled with them as they crossed the plain. The horsemen rode with the free, easy swing of the Spaniard, and their Spanish bits, saddles and huge *tapaderos* gave them the appearance of the vaqueros to be found farther to the south-west.

At their head rode a man of wide girth and broad shoulders, decked out in chaps and doublet of deerskin. It was Basil.

From under·the broad brim of his Spanish sombrero, his jovial eyes drank in the indolent charm of his rancho as his lazy servants, quickened to life at the sound of his coming, rushed forward with ingratiating bows to serve him.

At the steps of the spacious veranda, he suddenly stopped and peered down a path that led from the river.

He stood speechless as he saw coming toward him a weary old man with a girl trudging beside him. Slowly a light of joyous recognition illumined his eyes and he rushed forward with excited exclamations of welcome.

"Evangeline! Father Felician!" he shouted as he gathered them both into his huge arms in a bear-like embrace.

Tired from her long journey, but happy with expectancy, Evangeline snuggled close to Basil as Father Felician, beaming with joy, noted the change that had come over his old friend.

"Are you really Basil Lajeunesse?"

Father Felician laughed, "With all these Spanish trappings you seem more like some Don of old Spain than our Basil of Grand-Pré.

Basil laughed with his old time vigor.

"Talk not to me of Grand-Pré," he roared. "Here is a land that is better than the old one! No hungry winter freezes your blood, no field is filled with stones to break the back and the heart of the farmer. Why, the grass grows more in a single night than in a whole Canadian summer!"

"It is easy to see that you've prospered," nodded the *Curé*.

"Why not—with everything at hand to help you? Here land is to be had for the asking. My herds—I never have time to count them—run wild on the unfenced prairies. It takes only a few blows of the axe to fell timber enough for a mansion. Yes, and after your house is built there is no tyrant to drive you away from it or steal your crops and your cattle!"

The memory of his expulsion from Grand-Pré brought a snort of wrath to his nostrils.

"But enough of myself and this new land that I love. Welcome to you, my good friends . . . you who have so long been friendless and homeless! Tell me where you have wandered and how you came to find me!"

"It was in Saint Martin, where we found René and Baptiste and many of the others, that a hunter told us where we would find you."

Basil would have discussed their wanderings. Questions tumbled from his lips as he started to lead them to the house.

Evangeline slipped from his embrace and confronted him.

"Gabriel . . . where is Gabriel?" she asked.

Basil stood rooted in his tracks. Too late he remembered the long years of seeking that had driven his son up and down the rivers and finally taken him away to the mountains. His happiness of a moment before ran away from his face like water out of a basin.

Evangeline grasped his dismay immediately.

"He is not here?" she cried.

"If you came by the river and the bayous, how have you missed him?" he parried. "Even now he must be somewhere between here and the junction of the rivers."

Basil's surprise was as genuine as their dismay.

"Gone . . . Gabriel gone?"

Evangeline still was unwilling to believe his words. As she saw Basil nod, her over-burdened heart gave way and, unable to stand up under the crushing disappoint-ment, she buried her face on his bosom and wept.

Basil tried to console her, but her grief knew no stopping.

"Only yesterday Gabriel left for the Ozarks," said he. "Thinking ever of you, restless and troubled, no good to himself or to me, he went away, hoping in new lands to hear some word of you."

"If only we had hurried," Evangeline sobbed. "If we had not tarried so long in Saint Martin. . . ."

"Be of good cheer, Evangeline," Basil comforted her, caressing her cheek and smiling with broad reassurance, "to-mor-row at dawn we shall leave and overtake him. I will take my swiftest and lightest canoe. Father Felician can wait here until we return. I promise that if we have to go all the way to the mountains, I will find Gabriel for you."

Basil finally coaxed a smile to her lips and led them into the ranch-house, order-ing his servants to hasten the dinner, and brooking no delay with as imperious a man-

ner as ever he charged to the Governor-
General of Nova Scotia.

In the great living-room of the ranch-
house, with its comfortable Spanish furn-
ishings, she looked anxiously about for
trace of Gabriel's belongings.

"Here is his room," he suggested, and
led her to the door.

As she slipped inside, Basil turned to
Father Felician with a broad smile and a
knowing glance.

Just to be alone in the sweet intimacy of
Gabriel's room brought a flush to Evangeline's cheeks. Murmuring dreamily to herself, she moved about, touching with tender
affection the articles his hands had used so
often and finding little tokens that she
had given him back in the days when they
were children.

On the wall she discovered an old hunt-
ing jacket. She pressed her cheek to the
sleeve, and closing her eyes, tried to
imagine that his arm was in it and slowly
drawing her close to his side.

"Soon we shall be together, Gabriel,"
she mused. "Here, in this new land that
your father loves, we will be happy."

# CHAPTER XVII

### THE CROSS IN THE STORM

Basil sat up after supper talking over old times with Father Felician. He was delighted to find that René and his son and many of the others so well known to him were only a few days' journey away.

"I am glad that they have prospered," said he. "The faith that you taught us has been well rewarded."

"It will not have been in vain if we can bring Gabriel back to her," mused the *Curé*. "Her patience deserves the special dispensation of Providence."

"We shall find him," Basil reiterated, and he pounded the arm of his chair with his great fist. "I know the river as well as most. We will leave at dawn. By evening of the following day we should overtake him."

The preparations for their hurried departure were soon completed, and the next morning before the sun peeked over the

rim of the world, Evangeline and Basil arose
from the breakfast table and said farewell
to Father Felician. The *Curé* accompanied
them down to the water.

Basil stood with head uncovered as the
priest gave them his blessing. Evangeline
knelt in prayer.

"Be on your way," Father Felician ad-
monished finally. "See that you bring back
the truant lover."

Basil pushed the light canoe out into the
swift-moving stream. Raising his paddle,
he waved farewell. The current caught the
bark and in a few minutes a bend in the
river hid them from view.

The morning dispelled all doubt and
gloom from Evangeline's mind and she
smiled happily as Basil, puffing contentedly
at his pipe of sweet Natchitoches tobacco,
paddled the canoe far out into the stream.

Father Felician, sharing Evangeline's
confidence that the end of her search was
close at hand, stood long on the shore,
gazing, without realizing it, for the last
time at the departing form of the girl, following her with misty eyes as the little
craft melted away into the distance.

Though Evangeline and Basil followed

in swift pursuit of Gabriel, not that day, nor in many days, did they overtake him on lake or river. Always they came too late, finding only the dead ashes or embers of his deserted camp-fires.

But hope still guided her on . . . far into the Indian camps of the West, into the lumber camps of the North, back to the Ozark Mountains . . . a mirage that ever retreated and vanished before her.

Weeks became months, but always Basil said: "We shall find him."

Torrential rains overtook them in autumn, but unwilling to delay lest they lose all trace of Gabriel, they plunged on into the face of one raging storm after another.

In a trading-post on the Little Osage, Basil spoke to a half-breed who had just come up the river.

"Gabriel was camped beside me last evening," he declared.

Basil rushed to Evangeline with the good news.

"But this rain will keep us here over night," Evangeline argued.

"No!" Basil exclaimed vehemently. "No storm can hold us back now!"

So, risking the dangerous current of the

river, with its chutes of white water and jagged rocks, they flashed away from their camp-fire.

All day they were tossed perilously about on the swollen river. When night fell the storm increased in fury. Icy winds drove gusts of rain against their faces, white in the intermittent flashes of lightning.

"We dare not go on!" Evangeline screamed in Basil's ear to make herself heard above the thrashing of the trees and the roaring of the river.

"It's too late to risk making for shore," Basil shouted back.

Down the raging stream the canoe plunged in the terrifying darkness of the night, the lightning playing about them and the deafening rumble of thunder rising above the crashing of falling trees in the forest.

Stark and grim, drenched and blinded with rain, they fought desperately to keep the canoe from capsizing, working furiously with their paddles against the swirling rapids of the river.

Without warning, the canoe, caught in a treacherous whirlpool, crashed into a half-submerged rock. With a shriek of terror, Evangeline was hurled into the icy water.

Basil, clinging to the wreckage of the canoe, was swept downstream, his voice booming back to her through the darkness.

Desperately Evangeline managed to cling to a jutting rock, her numb fingers hardly able to grasp its slippery surface. Gaining strength, she pulled herself, inch by inch, out of the water and sank, exhausted, on the surface.

"Basil!" she called. "Basil!"

Downstream, puffing furiously, Basil pulled himself out on the opposite bank. He tried to scan the river for a trace of Evangeline.

Swaying dizzily, still dazed from the shock of her terrifying experience, Evangeline stumbled into the underbrush of the forest. Instinctively turning away from the rising river, groping blindly, the wind and rain slashing and whipping the reeds and saplings across her body and bleeding face, she went on.

Half crazed in the howling wind and the roaring thunder, she stumbled and fell headlong in the mud, only to rise again and desperately fight her way through the pitiless storm.

As though in supreme effort, the storm gods uprooted a forest giant. The great

tree tore a swath through the forest. A
limb struck Evangeline and bore her to the
ground, pinioning her beneath its heavy
branches. She tried desperately to free herself, working with hands and feet until exhausted.

Suddenly, in a flash of lightning, her
eyes opened wide with wonderment. Standing out in bold relief against the dark trunk
of a tree, she beheld a crucifix of the Christ.

Gazing transfixed at the cross, as though
viewing a miracle, Evangeline's strength
ebbed back. Bravely she struggled until she
freed herself. Half stumbling, half dragging herself, she fell at its base and clasped
her arms about its sacred trunk . . . a pitiful, pathetic figure in the beating, relentless
rain.

Basil fought his way back to the scene
of their accident. Wading out in the rush-
ing water until another step would have
left him at the mercy of the river, he waited
for the lightning to flash.

"She's gone!" he groaned as he beheld
the bare rock to which Evangeline had
clung.

"She's gone. . . ."

Minute after minute he stood in the cold,
whirling water, seeking in vain for some

sign of her lifeless body. At last, exhausted and broken, he stumbled ashore to follow the bank, staring into the darkness, hoping against hope that he might find her.

Morning dawned and the yellow flood of the river rushed on.

"She is dead!" he mumbled deliriously.

"Gabriel never will find her now!"

# CHAPTER XVIII

## SO SAINTS HAVE BEEN TRIED

With the dawn, a shaft of light pierced the boiling, black clouds of the storm, and Evangeline raised her bewildered eyes to the shining crucifix, a spiritual glow creeping over her fevered face. Into her consciousness stole the conviction that it was a sign from Heaven . . . an omen that her search for Gabriel must end.

An old Jesuit, called by the Shawnees The Black Robe, blinked his eyes in the sunlight as he opened the door of his mission to survey the damage the storm had done.

A smothered, startled cry escaped his lips as he discovered Evangeline, clinging to the trunk of the tree, her eyes gazing transfixed upon the cross.

Solicitiously the old missionary lifted her and carried her into the chapel. Evangeline pushed the damp, disheveled hair from her forehead and smiled wanly into his kindly face.

"We were capsized on the river," she explained. "I was thrown onto a rock and managed to cling there. Finally I made my way into the forest. But Basil . . . where is he? Was he saved, Father?"

"The Indians have found your battered canoe," the Jesuit hurried to answer, "but there is no word of him whom you call Basil."

Evangeline broke into a paroxysm of tears at this confirmation of her dread misgivings.

"It was my folly," she groaned, "refusing to be held back by storm or flood or fires in the forests . . . and now he is gone . . . a martyr to me and my love for Gabriel, his son."

The missionary's eyes lighted as he grasped the meaning of what she was telling him.

"Weeks ago I heard this same story from Gabriel's own lips," said he very solemnly. "It is strange! He sat beside me on this very mat and poured out just such a tale of feverish wandering and undying devotion."

A hundred times in her journeying had she felt her pulse quicken as some one told her of having spoken to Gabriel. She had always answered by plunging on in mad pursuit of him.

This morning the Jesuit's words failed to kindle the lamp of hope in her eyes. Instead, she slowly raised her face and gazed at the cross in silent meditation.

"I can not go on," she murmured weakly. "First the crucifix staring at me in the storm . . . and now the news of Basil's death! It can only mean that God does not wish me to find Gabriel."

The missionary smiled benignantly.

"Do not say that, my child. Thus have saints been tried . . . and not found wanting."

"Oh, let me remain here with thee, Father," she begged, trembling with a sob. "Let me remain . . . for my soul is sad and afflicted."

"There is need of you here, my child," said he. "You can work among the Indians, your sweet presence converting them where I might fail. Next Spring Gabriel will be returning on his way to the southland. Wait here and meet him."

So it was arranged, and in the quiet of the woods and affection of the Indian women and children among whom she toiled, Evangeline found peace of a kind.

Winter passed at last and Spring began
to call, even as Chopeesh, the bluebird, had
called to Glooskap.

One evening as she sat beside her fire, an
Indian woman entered the camp, in her
face traces of sorrow and patience as great
as Evangeline found in her own.

She was a Shawnee woman, returning
home from the far-off land of the Coman-
ches, where her husband, a French *coureur-
des-bois*, had been killed in a raid.

Evangeline's heart was touched by her
story. She bade her welcome and fed her,
a strange bond of affection drawing them
together.

As the Shawnee woman told her story,
Evangeline wept to know that another had
loved and had been disappointed; but glad
in her sorrow that the other one who had
suffered was near her that she might ease
her grief with kindness and affection.

Moved by pity and compassion, Evangeline repeated the story of her own unhappy
love. Long after she had finished, the
Shawnee maiden sat mute.

"It is like the tale of Mowis, the snow
bridegroom," she said at length, and pro-
ceeded to tell Evangeline the Shawnee
story of Mowis, who won and wedded a
maiden, but at dawn he rose and stole from

the lodge to fade and melt away in the sunshine. Although the maiden followed him deep into the forest, she never beheld him again.

"So have I followed Gabriel," Evangeline whispered.

As the season progressed and the wild flowers came to carpet the floor of the forest, the old urge to take up her search for Gabriel grew on her. For a week she refused to listen to the ever-insistent voice that tortured her.

At last, in a fever of desperation, she spoke to the missionary.

"Father, he has not come. Spring is almost gone."

The Jesuit was not surprised by her query. For days he had noticed her growing agitation.

"Yes, he is long overdue," he admitted. "Go, if the spirit moves you, my child."

"A Shawnee has described a trapper to me who lives on the Saginaw, near where it empties into Lake Huron," said Evangeline. "There will I go . . . and failing to find him, bow to the will of God and devote the rest of my life to His service."

So it befell that as Basil wandered back to his rancho to face the questioning eyes of Father Felician, Evangeline joined a party of guides returning to the St. Lawrence.

Weeks passed before she reached the end of her journey. In a rude camp on the banks of the Saginaw men told her that it was Gabriel Lajeunesse who trapped further up the river.

She hurried on, paddling her own canoe through the wilderness, strangely safe among rough men and war-like Indians.

At last she found the lodge for which she searched . . . found it to see it fallen to ruins and deserted.

She sought in the wreckage for some sign of Gabriel . . . and found nothing. Crushed, she turned away, raising her eyes to Heaven.

"This is Your answer . . . and I accept it," she moaned.

# CHAPTER XIX

"FATHER, I THANK THEE!"

In a narrow, winding street of Philadelphia, City of Brotherly Love, founded by William Penn, the apostle of kindness, the candles gleamed furtively as a silent little figure scurried by.

She nodded and spoke a soft word of greeting to the lamplighter and night-watchman.

The two old men lifted their hats and bowed to her, following her with their eyes as she disappeared into a dark doorway, their attitude plainly one of reverence.

A few moments later they saw a light illumine a garret window high up in the dark, dingy building she had entered.

"It's Evangeline, the little Sister of Mercy," said the lamplighter, and his wrinkled old face broke into a humble smile. "She is everywhere these days, administering to the poor and sick."

"I know her well," replied the watchman, and he nodded his head reminiscently to himself, for he had often encountered her meek, pale face in many parts of the city, late at night and in the graying dawn of the morning.

Humbly, with reverent steps, Evangeline had followed the feet of the Saviour. Though often lonely and wretched, she found an antidote for her misery in bringing comfort to the poor and forgotten.

In dingy attics, where distress and want concealed themselves from the sunlight, and disease and sorrow languished neglected, her brave, smiling face brought a benediction.

It was to Philadelphia that she had first come in the days of her exile. Gabriel had landed there, too. If they were ever to meet, she told herself, it must be in this city of elms.

Philadelphia was a town of importance even in that day. Men were always coming and going. Some day, Gabriel's straying feet must lead him there.

Thus, with patience and self-abnegation, happy in her devotion to others, Evangeline lived with the image of Gabriel engraved on her heart.

That winter a pestilence fell on the city. The rich could not escape it and the poor and the friendless crept away to die in the almshouse, home of the homeless.

A deep concern settled upon Philadelphia. In the common misfortune, the floodgates of brotherly love were opened, and those in high places were no longer scornful of the lowly.

To the house of the poor came the little Sister of Mercy. In her long, dark robes and surplice of white, she glided noiselessly through the doors and corridors, lined with the cots of the dead and the dying.

The poor, sick, friendless souls in pain and anguish, looked up into her face as she moistened their fevered lips, and thought to behold gleams of celestial light encircle her forehead, such as artists paint over the brow of the saints, while her presence fell on their hearts like a ray of sun on the walls of a prison.

As she passed from cot to cot, she saw how Death, laying his hand upon many a heart, had healed it forever.

Days crawled by. Every morning found many familiar faces missing. Evangeline knew accordingly that the grim reaper had not paused in his work during the night.

But as one weary soul disappeared, a

dozen came to take his place. She was bending over a lad to catch his last whispered words when a cry resounded throughout the ward.

"Evangeline . . . where are you?" it said.

Evangeline straightened up, her face transfixed.

"Who is it that calls for Evangeline?" she gasped.

On a pallet a few feet away, a man, his form wasted, his spirit almost exhausted, stirred and tried to raise himself. But death was too near, and he fell back motionless.

Hot and red on his lips burned the bright flush of fever. Evangeline came and gazed at him.

Suddenly arrested in wonder and fear, she stopped, her own colorless lips apart, while a shudder ran through her slender frame. Then a terrible cry of anguish fought its way through her tightening throat.

"Gabriel! . . . Gabriel, my beloved!" she moaned as she sank to her knees beside him.

At the sound of Evangeline's voice, tender and saintly, Gabriel opened his eyes. Recognizing her through the haze of approaching death, he vainly tried to speak, but the words died on his trembling lips and only their motion revealed what his tongue would have said.

"My love," she crooned. "At last I have found you!"

In a dream, Gabriel beheld the home of his boyhood . . . green Acadian meadows, surging sea and woodlands. And walking with him under the shadow of the pines and the hemlocks, as in the days of his youth, was Evangeline, fairest of all the maids of Grand-Pré.

"Do you know me, Gabriel?" she sobbed.

His eyes smiled back, and she knew that he recognized her.

"I . . . love . . . you," he managed to whisper. "Sing . . . to . . . me. . . ."

Tenderly, with infinite care, she cradled him in her arms and crooned the plaintive melodies she had sung to him in the days when romance was young in their hearts.

In the darkened chamber of sickness, the patients and attendants listened enraptured as though hearing the song of an angel from Heaven.

"He is dying," a doctor warned.

Evangeline nodded and sang on, her heart breaking.

Bravely, Gabriel tried to rally, but

slowly his head sank and Evangeline closed his lids in eternal slumber.

Tears streamed down her face as she raised her eyes to Heaven. Her lips quivered and in a voice spiritual and holy she murmured:

"Father, I thank Thee. . . ."

THE END